The depths of the ocean hide more secrets than one...

When a man without a memory washes up outside her lonely seaside cottage, Meg can't explain the connection she feels to him. She should be afraid, suspicious, even angry that he would disturb her hard-won peace. But something about Caleb Hunter calls to her. On instinct, Meg asks this stranger into her home, her life—into the place left vacant by her dead husband, who drowned at sea a year to the day before Caleb appeared.

But something isn't right. Half-buried memories begin to haunt Meg's dreams, Caleb seems to know things he can't possibly know, and there are signs that someone else is watching them, someone with a heart as cold as the sea...

I0677621

Books by Celia Ashley

Dark Tides

Published by Kensington Publishing Corporation

Dark Tides

Celia Ashley

LYRICAL PRESS
Kensington Publishing Corp.
www.kensingtonbooks.com

Lyrical Press books are published by
Kensington Publishing Corp. 119 West 40th Street New York, NY 10018

All Kensington titles, imprints, and distributed lines are available at special quantity discounts for bulk purchases for sales promotion, premiums, fund-raising, and educational or institutional use.

Special book excerpts or customized printings can also be created to fit specific needs. For details, write or phone the office of the Kensington Special Sales Manager:
Kensington Publishing Corp.
119 West 40th Street
New York, NY 10018
Attn. Special Sales Department. Phone: 1-800-221-2647.

First Electronic Edition: May 2015
eISBN-13: 978-1-61650-565-3
eISBN-10: 1-61650-565-6

First Print Edition: May 2015
ISBN-13: 978-1-61650-968-2
ISBN-10: 1-61650-968-6

Printed in the United States of America

To the ladies at PLRW—
thank you for your sisterhood

Author's Foreword

Although I have a love for the solitude of a barren coastline, the town in which my heroine lives is, of course, fictional, as are all the characters. That is not to say they do not live in my heart, because every character ever set to paper and fleshed out does live there, populating the worlds of my creation. There are those who have not yet been born, as well, but they are—quite literally—for another story.

Regarding the paranormal element of Dark Tides, I possess some personal experience in this area although not, of course, to the extent to which Meg and Caleb will experience the supernatural in the pages to follow. As with all writers, the ability to take an element of knowledge and expand it to take on another life entirely is our humble gift. I hope the sharing of this gift with you will be entertaining and maybe a little chilling, although ultimately hearts will be warmed.

As always, I am grateful to my readers for allowing my worlds into theirs. Thank you all.

Chapter 1

Swiping a handful of sodden hair from his eyes, Caleb Hunter scrambled upright, stepping away from the water purling around his bare feet. An expanse of sand stretched as far as he could see into a soaking fog, although beyond the crest of dune in front of him, a slate-roofed, decrepit white Victorian rose out of the shimmering haze. The house didn't look at all familiar. Neither did the beach. Nothing did, no matter what direction he turned.

With a deep, painful breath, Caleb considered what he did know. His name, for one. Good. He thought he might be thirty-five or thirty-six years old. Somehow, he knew he stood six-foot-one, he had brown eyes, and his nearly black hair badly needed trimming. At this point, it needed a great deal more than that, plastered with salt and sand and a bit of debris hanging in front of his eyes. Yanking a piece of seaweed from above his brow, he tossed the vegetation down, tracking its descent past the length of his naked body. He pivoted in a slow, searching circle. Not a stitch of clothing lay in the sand.

After a moment, he lifted his hands, turning them palm up and finding them well-formed, calloused across the pad of flesh below his fingers. The skin of his fingertips had wrinkled from long immersion, and fine sand had embedded in the bend of each joint. Salt and sand encrusted the hair on his chafed arms. A black, ugly bruise throbbed on his right forearm. When he flexed his hand, the injury burned deep into the muscle. More sand coated his torso and his groin, clumped in the hair on his legs, and grated in places more private. He planted his feet apart and bent to brush the sand away, discovering this only made the situation worse.

Dismayed by his lack of recollection, as well as his lack of garments, Caleb closed his eyes and pushed both hands through his hair. Clasping his fingers behind his neck, he frowned when he located a hard knot of tender flesh at the base of his skull. Something had struck him there. He remembered that.

No, not something. Someone. Someone had tried to kill him.

Shit.

That fragment of recall brought no further revelation, but his skin crawled in reaction to a danger he couldn't fathom, and he checked again to make certain no one else occupied the stretch of beach. Shredding fog revealed a woman approaching him from a short distance. Walking with her head down, she bent every now and then to collect small items from the water's edge. Not knowing what else to do, Caleb sat in the sand once more, pulling his knees up close to his chin and wrapping his arms around his legs. After ascertaining he'd tucked everything neatly out of view, he waited.

She stopped little more than a dozen feet from him, bending to pluck at a polished stone to deposit with the array of minuscule treasures on her palm. The wind fluttered the length of a dark blue shawl from her shoulders, dragging the fringed edge in the sand. Tan trousers, rolled to the knee, exposed the curve of her calf and slender feet washed by the surge of the tide as she crouched. Caleb lifted his gaze again to her face. Even at that distance, he could see her eyes were quite green and staring straight into his.

Clutching her treasure trove against her breast, the woman straightened. Her lips moved in speech, words drowned by the low growl of the tide. Caleb cleared his parched throat, uncertain what to say as the woman continued to stare at him with an unreadable expression. After a moment, she dropped the items from her fingers into a heap on the sand and backed away, placing one bare foot behind the other, gaze never leaving his face until she turned on her heel and started an awkward run across the shifting sand. The blue shawl flew from her shoulders.

Leaping to his feet, Caleb darted forward and snatched up the garment, draping the soft wool around his waist. He tugged the folds to cover as much of his hip area as he could. Scooping the woman's discarded treasure into his hand, he went after her, following her toward the white house. Already a good distance ahead of him, she leaped up the long flight of wooden steps from the beach two at a time, crossing a seaside garden to a porch, where she yanked open the door and disappeared inside. Caleb paused in uncertainty. He hadn't meant to alarm her, and she appeared frightened, not merely startled. Nevertheless, if he didn't speak to her, he had no hope of receiving any answers to his many questions.

Girding his determination, as well as his grip on her shawl, he set his own bare feet to the first step and climbed to a brick pathway that led through the garden. At the porch, he paused again, studying the length of the covered area, the blank face of each window for any sign she peered out at him. He found only the milky reflection on glass of the fogged-in sea.

He walked across the porch and halted in front of the door. "Hello?" he called, listening hard.

She responded in a muffled demand through the solid wood. "Who are you?"

"I'm sorry if I startled you."

Silence.

"My name is Caleb Hunter," he said with a crazy expectation she would throw open the door and announce him welcome, perhaps apologize for not recognizing him in his present state. Instead, he heard nothing. The door remained closed.

"I need help." He waited. "I thought I would return your shawl to you, but…but I have a specific need of it at the moment."

"Keep it," he heard her say. The fact she had spoken again gave him a glimmer of hope.

"I don't know where I am," he persisted. "I don't know who I am," he added, frowning down at the worn boards of the porch floor. Aloud, the statement sounded ludicrous. The brief flare of fear surging through him at his own words held no humor at all.

"What do you mean, you don't know who you are?"

The door creaked open. A security chain stretched taut in the space between frame and door. Her leaf-green eyes regarded him intently from behind a fringe of honey-colored bangs.

"I don't remember much of anything specific," he said. "I believe I was hit on the head and…and maybe I washed up onto the beach from the ocean. I'm not sure. My name is about all I do remember with any certainty. Is the name Caleb Hunter familiar to you?"

"No," she said. "I don't know anyone by that name."

The door shut again. Scoured by the salt winds, the light blue paint had peeled away in places to show the bare, weathered wood beneath. A moment later, the door opened again, enough for her to toss something out at him. He bent and picked up a crumpled pair of pants. Light blue fabric, heavy and faded with wear. Jeans, they were called. He remembered that. They looked like they would fit him.

Turning his back, Caleb dropped the shells, stones, and bits of sea glass onto the lacquered surface of a nearby wicker chair. He set the shawl beside them and hastened into the jeans, grimacing as sand abraded his flesh. If the woman still stood in the doorway watching him struggle with the pants, she gave no indication. He glanced over his shoulder. Through the narrow opening, he saw nothing.

"What was that in your hand?"

At her question, he slowly pivoted to face the door, feeling more naked now than he had in her shawl. Talking to her half-dressed, wearing nothing but a pair of borrowed blue jeans, he contemplated picking up the shawl and draping it across his shoulders. Instead, he seized it from the floor where it had fallen and placed it beside her rescued treasure. The door opened a little more and her face appeared.

"Your things," he said by way of explanation. "I never meant to frighten you, to make you drop what you'd been gathering."

She frowned at the shells and oddments he had placed on the chair before turning her gaze to meet his. Slow to speak, she studied him a moment. "Thank you."

The door closed again.

Caleb moved to another chair and sat down. He leaned forward, elbows on thighs, hands folded together between his knees. The shifting of his body renewed pain in every muscle and tendon. Reaching up, he fingered the back of his head to trace again the contours of the vicious lump. He remembered a flurry of fists, grunting blows, and male voices raised in harsh invective, but he didn't recall the words. Was one of those voices his? Could have been. Yes, it could have been his voice. He remembered…nothing. Nothing else.

Damn it.

Once more, the door opened. The woman stepped onto the porch holding out a T-shirt. Gratefully, he took it, then slipped the garment over his head. It smelled as if it had been left sitting in a drawer. Not that it mattered.

"Your husband's?" he asked, not certain from what part of his brain such a question came.

She nodded.

"Is he here?"

"He's dead," she said.

"Oh." Caleb ran his hand through his salt-encrusted hair. "I'm sorry."

"So am I."

She moved to the chair where her shawl lay and bent to pick up the items he had deposited there. Brushing the sand and crushed shell from the seat into her hand as well, she walked to the porch railing and sprinkled them into the garden below, permitting them to flow through a loose fist. Her eyes closed as she did this, as if something ritualistic existed in the execution of her action. He wondered what had happened to her husband, if maybe she did this in his memory.

"His ship went down in a storm."

He started, meeting her eyes. Her direct gaze made him shiver.

"That's what you were thinking, wasn't it?" she said, brushing her hands clean. "You were wondering how he died."

Caleb shivered again within the confines of a dead man's shirt. "Yes," he admitted, "I was."

She nodded, her longs bangs swinging forward. "A year ago today," she told him quietly.

Today. Caleb said nothing.

She moved back across the porch, stopping before the chair opposite him where she gathered up the shawl and sat, holding the garment balled against her stomach. With her feet tucked around the outside of the legs of the chair, knees angled together, she appeared innocent and vulnerable. Caleb's stomach churned. He shoved a fist against his abdomen in an effort to control the response.

"I dream about him most nights," she confided in a voice barely above a whisper, her eyes intent on his own. "But not always. This morning, though, on the anniversary of his death, I dreamed about someone else. I didn't realize it until I saw you on the beach. I'm fairly certain I dreamed of you."

Stunned by her speech, Caleb sat back hard against the chair frame. His breath exploded as the knot at the base of his skull met wood, causing him to jerk forward again, bright pinpoints of light dancing before his eyes.

He couldn't remember the fundamental particulars about himself and his life, but he knew what dreams were without requiring an explanation. What she said made no sense to him. None at all. Unless—

"What do you mean? Do you know me?" he asked again. Perhaps she didn't know his name, but she might recall having seen him somewhere. Something. Anything.

She raised her eyes from a fierce contemplation of the air between them. After a moment of consideration, she shook her head. He licked his dry, salty lips as he shifted on the seat, frowning at the pain wracking his body. Observing his movements, she reached into her pocket and drew out a narrow black object, holding it on her palm. From somewhere in the recesses of murky recognition, he recognized a cell phone. "What are you doing?"

"Calling the police," she said.

Don't let her. Don't let her. Don't let her.

The force of the voice in his head caused him to gasp, recognizing without understanding that an instinct for preservation spoke to him. "Don't," he said and added "please" more sedately at the widening of her eyes.

She displayed no further consternation at his command, just cocked her head to the side, her gaze turning contemplative as if studying him. Even so, he could see the pulse beating beneath her jaw, the momentary suspension of her respiration.

"Why not?" she asked after a moment, still holding the phone at the ready in her hand.

He tried to dredge up a reply she would find suitable. He couldn't imagine where to begin. "God, I don't know," he answered, lowering his head into his hand, shoving fingers deep into his tangled hair. "I don't. I don't know. I...I don't know."

He heard a short, decisive inhalation and looked up in time to witness her returning the phone to her pocket. Fingers curled loosely, she lowered her right hand into her left across her stomach. "Don't you want to go to the hospital?"

"Why?"

"Aren't you hurt?"

She waited for his reply. Caleb didn't believe he'd ever seen eyes so green, though he couldn't recall for certain. He straightened in the chair, folding his hands in his lap. "What makes you think I'm hurt?"

Blowing out a breath, she stood, tucking the sand-spattered shawl against her abdomen. "You can hardly move," she said. "And the wound to your head—"

"How do you know I have a head wound?"

Her mouth twisted in wry amusement. "I could say I dreamed it, but I didn't. You told me you thought you'd been hit on the head. Even if you hadn't, you wince every time you touch the back of your skull. That and the fact you can't remember who you are are fairly good indicators of some sort of head trauma. Which," she added, "is why you should have a doctor check you out. Even if you don't want the police involved, I could call an ambulance or, well, I suppose I could drive you to the hospital myself."

Possessing a certain amount of defiance in her expression, she did not look away from him. Her stance shifted, and her hand lifted to assist him in rising. He wondered at her trust in a stranger, standing so close to him with her hand extended, as if she had no idea how easily he could overpower her if he had the inclination. He could remember nothing about his past life. For all he knew, he could be a nasty sort of person, a dangerous man. After all, someone had tried to kill him, hadn't they? Somebody must have had good reason for that.

"Not yet," he whispered. His aversion to the possibility of questions, of a need for answers he could not provide, worried him. Was he taking a foolish risk, not getting medical help? Still, he didn't think his injuries were life threatening. He felt no weakness, no disorientation beyond his inability to recall.

"You could be bleeding internally. You could have a skull fracture."

He rubbed his eyes, sand grating across his lids. "Are you suggesting I might die?"

"I don't know," she said. "I'm not a doctor."

Through the slats of the porch railing, he saw the sea, the fog lifting above the waves. Possibly, he'd walked to the beach from somewhere else and collapsed here, but that didn't seem likely. In fact, he knew better. The sensation of plunging into the ocean, tumbling through the cold, salty tides, though not quite memory, had the resonation of truth.

"I know a doctor who will come to the house. I've had him here before. He is…well, discreet. At least he can check you out, and if he feels you need to go to a hospital, you will. If not, well, that's up to you then."

Up to him. What would he do if this doctor pronounced him well enough to avoid treatment? How would he even begin to know what steps to take next? Avoiding thought of all the unimaginable possibilities, he nodded at her. "Fine," he said. "Let him come."

She walked to the far side of the porch, talking into the instrument she'd pulled back out of her pocket, glancing at him over her shoulder as she spoke. After a few minutes, she returned. "He'll be here shortly. You may as well wait inside."

He eyed her with bewilderment. "You're not afraid to have me in your house?"

"Should I be?"

"I don't know."

"I do." She held out her hand again. Swallowing, he slipped his fingers into hers and allowed her to pull him up from his seat with surprising strength. Standing before her, he smelled the sea in her hair, the fresh air, and a faint suffusion of citrus. The top of her head barely came up to his collarbone. A feeling of protectiveness stole over him, making him frown.

"Are you sure you don't know me?" *Because it sure as hell feels like I know you.*

"Positive," she said. "And by the way, my name is Meg. Meg Donovan." Clutching the shawl in her fist, she headed inside, leaving the door standing wide. Confounded, Caleb followed her into the house, the inside of his borrowed pants chafing like sandpaper over thighs and calves and along the tender flesh of his testicles. He trailed her from the back door into the kitchen, where she indicated he should sit in a chair she slid from the table. She pulled back the curtains to allow more light into the room and walked behind him across worn linoleum to take a glass down from a cabinet. Outside the window, he saw the sun had broken through the fog, golden light reflecting in a shimmer on the pale blue ceiling of the porch. She opened the refrigerator and rummaged around inside before returning to stand beside him.

"Here," Meg said, handing him a glass of something orange. Orange juice. Yes, he remembered that. "Drink it slowly. Are you warm enough? I can get you a blanket if you need one. Sometimes shock—"

"I'm fine," he said.

"Hardly."

Circling around the table, she pulled out a chair on the opposite side and sat, folding her hands on the scarred painted surface. "So you know your name."

He nodded.

"Amnesia is a fascinating condition," she went on. "Not to you, I'm sure, but it's odd what the brain might pick and choose in terms of recollection. I'm thinking in the most severe cases, you wouldn't be able to walk or communicate or even pick up that glass, but I could be wrong."

Mulling over her words as he took several sips from the glass, he welcomed the slightly acidic burn in his throat. He set the glass down. "So you're saying I'm not too bad off, even though I can't remember a single goddamn thing except my name?"

"But that's not exactly true, is it?" Her gaze held his until she rose and stepped away from the table, leaving to answer a distant knock on another door. He clutched the glass of juice in both hands on the tabletop, staring past to a series of lines scratched into the table's wooden surface.

Not random, but seeming to spell out a word, a word he couldn't focus on as he thought about what she had said. How did she know? How did she know about the jumble of thoughts he held inside this fragile bubble in his mind?

"Caleb Hunter?" a deep voice said. "I'm Dr. Redecker, and I hear you may need my help."

Caleb spun on the chair to face the man standing between him and the interior kitchen door with a vague hope the man's face would be familiar. The gray hair, heavy countenance, and steady blue gaze meant nothing to him. This total lack of recollection made him understand something else, something he hadn't understood earlier. When looking into the eyes of the woman in whose kitchen he sat, he didn't see a stranger.

Chapter 2

Meg observed the doctor's examination of the man in her kitchen as he conducted a series of clinical tests for concussion, examined him for further injury, checked his vitals, and palpitated his abdomen and other areas for tenderness. Caleb Hunter tolerated the process with an appearance of strained patience, looking as though he wanted to be left alone. What Meg wanted was an assurance he wasn't going to die.

When he had completed his exam, Dr. Redecker stepped back, looking Caleb in the eye. "You don't show general confusion, just a specific lack of recall. There is a difference. You are battered and bruised, but not broken, although your head injury may be more than I can determine from my examination here. I would suggest a trip to the hospital—"

"No."

"Young man—"

"No, thank you," Caleb said.

"Then I have done what I can," Dr. Redecker muttered, closing his medical bag. "Rest your brain. That is no joke. No reading, no computer, no television, no work."

Caleb frowned.

"I guess that last goes without saying until you remember more details of your life," the doctor continued. "I will say nothing of this visit to anyone, but I strongly urge you to contact the police. They may be able to help you. If your symptoms worsen, you must go to the hospital. In the meantime, rest, and I will check on you in a few days' time."

Caleb lifted his head. "Rest where?"

"A hospital bed would be most appropriate. Since you have refused that advice, I can only say I don't know."

Shaking and releasing Caleb's hand, Dr. Redecker turned to head in Meg's direction.

"Let me get my checkbook," she said to him, pushing off from the counter.

He waved a hand in dismissal. "I'll forward the bill. When he remembers who he is, he can pay. The shelter still operates at the far side of town. Maybe you can take him there."

Meg nodded, thanking the doctor again before walking him to the front door. Upon her return, Caleb had not moved except to turn his head once more in the direction of the window. She studied his profile, the curve of his eyelid down to the crow's feet at the corner, the length of lash, dark and thick, the purpled line of his jaw, the slight arch of his nose as if it might have been broken at some point in his past. This was what she did, studied faces and drew them, painted them, fit them into illustrations in such a manner as to depict emotion and action. She saw none of that in his face at the moment, only an inability to move and a reverberating emptiness.

"Caleb."

He turned slowly at the sound of his name, recalled from the echoing void.

"You can stay here for a few days."

He shook his head. "I don't—"

"Yes," she said. "There is a guest room you can use. I have a lock on my bedroom door. I'm not worried."

"But maybe you should be."

Meg narrowed her eyes in study of the earnestness of his expression. "Why?"

"I don't know. It seems sensible, though."

"And yet..."

"And yet what?" he said with a deepening of the furrows on his brow.

"And yet I know things sometimes. I'm not worried."

Crossing the kitchen, Meg headed for the back stairs to the floor above. She paused to pick up a book off the lowest step and clutched it against her breast.

"But you don't know me," he said.

Looking back, she found him seated in the same position, hands between his thighs, watching her.

"I told you I don't," she answered.

"And I have to believe that."

"What choice do you have?"

He conceded the validity of her question with a flicker of his gaze. "Do you often dream of people you don't know?" he asked, the tone and phrasing of the query harsh. Meg frowned.

"I'm sorry," he went on, "but I don't think I'm mistaken in believing that dreaming of someone, then having them turn up on your doorstep, or at the very least the beach leading to your doorstep, is not a usual occurrence."

"I dream a lot."

"Of people you don't know," he persisted.

"Of many things."

"And these things you dream of come true? In some way, they come to pass?"

"Sometimes," she said, "yes, they do."

"Why do you think that is?"

For someone so befuddled by lapses in memory, his intellectual functioning did not seem impaired. Meg tightened her grip on the book, the edge of the cover pressing into her fingers. She drew a deep breath and then another.

"I wish to God I knew," she said. "It's hard when you don't know which of the things you see will happen and which will not. You end up jumping at shadows, trying to foresee everything, then you ignore it all, hoping it's meaningless, unable to recognize the one dream you should have paid attention to."

Picking up his glass of juice, Caleb drained the remnants. "And what did you dream about me?" he asked, his voice muffled against the back of his hand as he wiped pulp from his lip. "Something that might help me, do you think?"

Leaning against the doorframe, Meg let the book slide to her waist as she tried to recall. "I don't remember, exactly," she said, unable to find the details. "I had no recollection of having dreamed at all until I saw you. Only then did I know I hadn't dreamed of Matt this morning, of all mornings."

"Matt?" he echoed, his face contorting. "That was your husband's name?"

"It still is his name," she answered. "He didn't suddenly become nameless just because he died."

"I…of course not."

Meg nodded, the tiny movement tossing her bangs into her eyes. She blinked at the intrusion of hair into her lashes, at the sudden moisture blurring her gaze. She had to stop talking, lest she let loose something she would regret.

"You should rest for a little while," she said after a silent interval. "I'll put a towel and some more clean clothes for you in the bathroom and turn down the spare bed. I suppose lying down won't do you any harm, even if you do doze off. I'll wake you up regularly, if it comes to that, to make sure you're okay. You can shower and do whatever you need to do while I'm gone."

"Gone?" he said, rising from his seat, disheveled and wounded and wearing her dead husband's clothes. "Where are you going?"

"After I get you those things I promised," she said, "I'm going back to the beach. Maybe something else washed up besides you."

* * * *

The sun had come out, heating the sand beneath her feet as she walked up from the shoreline. She'd seen no evidence of shipwreck, no clothing, no wallet, no personal items at all except for a leather watch band, which, by the looks of it, had been in the ocean far longer than Caleb Hunter.

Halfway between the tide and the steps leading to the house, Meg sat in the sand. She drew her knees up. Curving her hands around her ankles, she stared out to sea, to the rocky channel, the lighthouse, and the horizon that stretched to forever, a boundary almost indistinguishable between ocean and sky. Thinking of the vastness of the ocean, the unknown depths, the lonely, lonely stretches of open water, she felt light-headed and frightened. She had never fully understood how men so loved the sea they gave up all for her. Well, not men in general. She didn't particularly care about the motivations of the sea-faring sector of the population. Only Matt. Matt who would always have been a wanderer, perhaps would have been destined to drive a truck over the road or something similar had he been born and raised somewhere inland rather than within the surging, siren call of the tides.

A year ago today—a day very like this one, the sun bright, temperature mild after a foggy morning—she'd answered a knock on her front door. The dying leaves on the bushes, flanking the entrance, had flamed gold in the afternoon light. The edge of Dan Stauffer's badge affixed to his shirtfront had glinted with fire as he stood beside the Coast Guard officer. Dan had watched her closely as he delivered the news, expecting shock, no doubt, and sorrow, despite the nearly two years Matt had been gone. Or perhaps he'd merely been looking for confirmation, in some fashion, of the wild rumors circulating about Matt since he'd left her and moved farther up the coast to continue his fishing operations.

Fishing…right. The rumors spoke of more than fishing. Hearing them, she'd been saddened more than surprised. She'd prayed they weren't true. Restless, discontented Matt with his rash schemes and his silent, smoldering rages, a criminal? She would have expected proof to be easily uncovered, if even half of the stories circulating had any basis in fact. Now, of course, none of them would ever know. The investigation had stopped with Matt's death. As for the pain and useless, stupid guilt that had punctuated the last years of married life? Well, it seemed to her Matt's death had only made it worse.

Lifting her face to the late autumn sun, she thought of the stranger she had left in her house, giving him free rein to go where he pleased, to steal from her if he chose, to lie in wait for her return. He could be shamming memory loss. The only thing he couldn't lie about were his injuries. Or the look in his eyes. The images she had seen there appeared in her own mind with such vivid clarity.

Confusing images nevertheless, images that could give him no peace. She did not believe him to be lying, did not sense any danger in his presence. But could she trust herself anymore? Trust the innate sense she had relied on so often in her life? She had not seen Matt's ship going down. Had not seen it at all, yet it had, vanishing into the dark depths of the ocean.

With a sigh, Meg yanked her ankles closer, gazing toward the horizon. Always capricious, the sea. When she chose to give up her carefully guarded secrets, there was no telling where they would come ashore. Ever.

In the town, at its highest point above sea level, stood a single stone cross with a brass plaque beneath. Every year new names of the sailors who did not return were added to the plaque. If she walked far enough up the beach, she would see the tip of the cross and the spire of the church at Church and Center Streets. Somewhere northeast of the town, and many nautical miles out to sea, lay Matt's body, or what remained after the creatures of the deep had finished with it. Lying with the others, bones scattered to the ocean floor for degeneration by the salt and the relentless motion of the water. She didn't like to think of it, didn't like to dwell on Matt's fate, his drowning. She hoped for his sake that everything had been over quickly, that one moment he'd been alive and filled with the hope of survival, and the next done, finished, drowned, without ever feeling any fear between.

Yet, he would have understood his chances and faced the inevitable with the harsh philosophy coloring everything he undertook, all the choices in his life. Fear might not have been a part of it. In later times, before the end, he used to tell her that the act of living itself was a risk, that pain and death were always right there waiting. As if she needed reminding.

She lowered her lids against the glare of the sun. The constant sea breeze tugged at her hair, loosening strands from the barrette at the back of her head. She breathed in and out, evenly, deeply, trying to banish the emotion pushing toward the surface. Gulls circled overhead, crying in the wind, waiting for a scrap or two of food she did not possess to offer. The waves crashed against the wet sand of the shoreline, curling and foaming, the beach empty, as it often was at this time of year. Late October weather could be unpredictable. Freak storms came up without warning, and the month was often too warm for the cold and ice and bitter winds that gave sailors and fishermen pause to return to hearth, home, and safety.

"Oh, Matt," she whispered. She pressed her forehead onto her knees, squeezing her eyes shut. Always going after what he wanted, no matter the consequences. Conscience be damned. Once, he'd possessed a gentler soul. She hardly remembered that man anymore.

She heard Caleb coming through the sand a few minutes later, a hitch to his step, the drop to his knees next to her causing a deadened thud of reverberation in her hips. He smelled ridiculously like her lavender soap and detergent, making him familiar to her when he should not have been at all.

"Are you all right?"

At the tone of concern from this wounded, troubled man, Meg bit her lip, willing herself not to weep. She would not. Not for everything she'd lost, for everything she'd bartered away in an attempt to keep a man who had not wanted her after all.

"I expect I'm a good deal better than you are," she said.

To her surprise, Caleb chuckled in response. He wriggled himself around until he'd imitated her position, gazing out toward the steel gray ocean. Thinking they had a new target for scraps, gulls circled close again, voices shrill.

"Did you find anything?"

Meg sat a minute longer without answering, feeling the balance of the shifted earth settle back into place. Struggling to her feet in the sliding sand, she brushed the clinging grains from her pants before shoving her hands deep into her pockets to still their trembling.

"I'm sorry, but I found nothing. That doesn't mean something might not wash up tomorrow or the next day or even a month from now."

He remained seated, his gaze intent, trying by dint of will to get her to look at him. But she would not look at the man she remembered vaguely from that place between slumber and waking, wouldn't look at the stranger whose scattered memories winked in and out of her mind with alarming intimacy.

"Hopefully a month from now such evidence will be moot," he said. "I can only trust I will remember everything by then."

"Hopefully," she agreed.

"I don't want the police involved. Not yet."

"I understand," she answered.

"Do you?"

She nodded. She remembered how their questions made her seem suspect rather than a willing participant in an investigation. Of course, she hadn't been entirely willing or cooperative. It had been Matt they were investigating.

"You should put ice on your head," she said. "See if the swelling goes down. Dr. Redecker said that would be good."

"Okay," he said. "Anything else?"

She considered a moment. "Other things will bring on amnesia," she said slowly, carefully. "Things too horrible to face."

"Is that what the doctor said?"

"No," she whispered. "That's what I say."

He lurched forward with an abrupt, awkward movement and froze, eyes wide in a troubled expression, almost as if he knew what she could see shimmering in the air, fleeing through her mind, turning on the edge of awakening. Matt, she recalled, had been afraid of her extrasensory recognition. Perhaps Caleb was, too.

He tipped his chin toward the sky, dark hair lifting in the breeze. Black-lashed tea-brown eyes narrowed against a swirl of sand he attempted to deflect with his hand as he regarded her solemnly. An attractive man, Caleb Hunter, lean and solidly built, his handsome face marked not only by bruising, but also by the evidence of a life lived, even if he could not remember it. The furrows beside his eyes spoke of days squinting in the sun, of concentration and deep passions. Yes, a very attractive man, who she had agreed to let sleep in a bed two doors down from her own.

She exhaled at the same instant he did. The tension left his shoulders. His hand dropped with a slap against his thigh. "All right."

Crossing her arms over her chest, Meg started back toward the house that had been hers and Matt's, where she had lived for three years without him since the day he had walked out with no intention of coming home.

For all of her reliance on this stupid inner sense of hers, she hadn't been a particularly good judge of Matt's character in the end.

As she climbed the weathered wooden staircase, she paused to look back. Caleb had not followed but had risen and moved to stand above the tide line, watching the sea.

Chapter 3

Meg cooked him dinner. He hadn't expected that, although he didn't know what he would have eaten had she not troubled to feed him. The food tasted fresh and delicately seasoned, and he wondered what he had been eating lately that forced him to make an unfavorable comparison to any unknown, recent meals. Following cleanup, she had gone about her business much as usual, he expected, in a room off the living room filled with paints and canvas, sketches, brushes, and pencils, sitting down before an easel where a painting rested, not yet completed. The light had faded rapidly from the autumn sky, necessitating the use of a lamp affixed to the top of the easel. He had the feeling he had kept her from performing this work at a more opportune time, but she did not say so.

He watched for a moment, frowning at the dark depiction of the sea, the tide executed in gradations of purple, midnight blue, and blood red, the sky above a mass of storm clouds in varying shades of gray. The picture disturbed him.

Leaving her to her work on the unsettling painting, he went into the living room, seeking distraction. There, he found a variety of children's books with her name as illustrator on the cover of each, although the authors varied. In light and evocative watercolors, she had created beautiful scenes of wildlife and snowfalls, of children and young animals, of gardens and mountains and ancient, gnarled trees from which swings hung drifting in the breeze. Studying the pictures, he understood Meg had been happy once. Clearly, by the painting in her studio, she wasn't now.

Caleb flipped through the pages of a book he had removed from a stand that was centered on the bookshelf—a recently published work, as the year of copyright on the front page coincided with the calendar he had seen hanging in the kitchen. Carefully, he put the volume back where he had found it. Turning to move on, he stopped at a clatter of falling objects from the nearby room.

"Are you all right?" Caleb called out.

Meg appeared on the threshold, standing on one foot as she leaned into the room, wiping her hands with a paint-smeared rag. He could smell something pungent coming from the cloth and wrinkled his nose.

"Turpentine," she said. "Paint thinner. Hard on the hands, but gets the paint off."

He nodded.

"I'll be finished in here in a minute."

"Don't stop because of me. I've just been looking at your books." He pointed to the nearest. Her gaze darted in the direction he pointed, her expression altering. He couldn't read the change, and in the next instant, it was gone, reverting to the smile she'd been wearing when she came in. He frowned.

"Be right out."

As soon as she disappeared, he continued his circuit around the room, picking up objects for a brief examination and putting them back down. He paused in front of an old hutch, his attention caught by the worn, barn-red doors. Grabbing the painted knob on the right side, he pulled the door open to reveal a column of drawers, each with a scarred, brass keyhole. Meg's light footsteps tapped across the hardwood floor behind him.

"This feels familiar," he said, without turning. "Is it a common type of furniture?"

She stepped past him, closing the door with a definitive click of the latch. "There's nothing in there."

"I wasn't...I wasn't asking." Yet he felt like perhaps he had been. "It was just...well, it seemed I'd seen something like it before."

"That's entirely possible. Probably not one exactly like this, but it is, as you said, a common type of furniture."

He continued to gaze at the shut door, visualizing the drawers behind it. He imagined they held all sorts of personal items, hints at a life, records and receipts and so many things he couldn't put a name to, things he almost remembered, sitting hidden from light at the edge of thought.

"Caleb? Are you all right?"

He grunted.

"Have you been reminded of something?"

"I think so. I think maybe I had a hutch. That's what it's called, right? I think I had one in the life I can't remember." She looked at him with sympathy before she touched his arm in reassurance and turned away.

I don't want your pity.

Shocked by the vehemence of his reaction, he clenched his hands into fists on the denim covering his thighs. A moment later, he scented the fragrance of her hair as she returned. She closed her fingers over his, pulling his left hand up between both of hers. "It'll be all right, Caleb. I don't know when. Just believe it will."

He met her gaze in defiance of the confusion that dashed with glancing blows around his brain, unable to believe anything would ever be all right.

* * * *

Lying in the dark, Caleb stretched in the confines of the narrow bed. He tucked his arms behind the upper part of his head, avoiding the goose egg. His gaze followed the shadowed path of a late moth across the ceiling. He had slept for a little while and then had come fully awake, with no idea of the time. In his disorientation, he could have been sleeping for hours or a handful of minutes. Somehow, though, he had the feeling he'd woken in the middle of the night.

Across the hall and down one door was her bedroom, by day a light-filled chamber with most of the lace-covered windows facing the ocean. When he had come up to shower, he had remained in the doorway for an inordinate amount of time, studying the accoutrements, the personal items scattered about—books and discarded clothing—the arrangement of furniture, the painted cast iron bed, the pair of dressers, a small desk in the corner, a worn, overstuffed chair in need of reupholstering. After, he had turned away, feeling guilty for his curiosity.

He wondered now if she slept untroubled or if she lay in her bed awake and uneasy with his presence in her house. He certainly would not blame her, knowing he occupied the room nearby, a stranger not only to her, but also to himself.

Letting his breath out, he closed his eyes and visualized Meg Donovan against his lids. Small in stature, she possessed an artless grace, moving restlessly from location to location as if she had no more weight or substance than one of the leaves in the breeze outside the window. It didn't matter if she was drawing the blinds or rinsing paint from a brush or rising up onto her toes before the bathroom mirror to comb her hair.

Ah, yes, well, he hadn't meant to walk in on her then. He had turned the corner to go into the bathroom and found her there, right in front of him. Although wearing thin and ratty sweatpants and an oversized T-shirt, she may as well have been naked. Dressed for bed, she would have walked out of the bathroom and into her bedroom, where she would have climbed beneath the mounded covers. During her marriage to her husband, they had most likely engaged in intimacy in that bed. He didn't want to think about it, yet he kept doing exactly that, visualizing Meg and a faceless man who occasionally appeared in his mind's eye bearing his own.

Disgusted with himself, he took to watching the moth again, gray-winged in the silver night. Despite the autumnal chill, he had lifted the sash an inch so he could hear the constant rhythm of the surf against the sand. Nearer, hot water ticked through the pipes of the old radiator. Fluttering erratically, the moth moved toward the open door and out the narrow space between the door and jamb. A shadow passed in the hall.

Sitting bolt upright, Caleb suppressed a groan as his pain-racked body protested the sudden movement. In the shower, he had located additional bruises on his torso and limbs, and all were bringing him noticeable discomfort. Swinging his feet over the side of the single bed, he snatched the borrowed blue jeans from the footboard. After tugging them on, he stepped shirtless into the corridor.

The half moon shining through the window at the far end illuminated an empty hallway. In silence, Caleb strode along the worn runner toward the sound of someone descending the stairs with quiet steps. Glancing at Meg's door, he saw it remained shut. Not her, then. His body tensed.

Taking the back stairs swiftly in his bare feet, he crept into the kitchen. Someone, or something, moved across the floor. The hair lifted along his arms.

The light went on. He squinted against the sudden, fluorescent glare.

"Caleb, I'm sorry, did I wake you? I tried not to make any noise."

"I wasn't asleep," he answered, more gruffly than he intended. "I thought someone had broken in."

She arched an eyebrow at him. Her hair, sleep-tousled, or perhaps from the restless lack of slumber, lay tangled about her shoulders. "And you were coming to do battle with the intruder. That's quite gallant of you. I'm glad it was only me."

Conscious of how foolish he must look, shirtless and unarmed, he sat down in the nearest chair. "You couldn't sleep either, I see," he said.

She gave him a strange look but nodded. "Would you like a glass of warm milk? It does work, you know. I'm making myself one."

"Warm milk?"

"To help you sleep."

"To help me sleep," he repeated, catching the flying edge of memory, of a slender hand pouring the steaming white contents of a pot into a mug. "Sure," he said. "Thank you."

He watched as she set about her preparations, pouring milk into an enameled pot, placing two mugs on the counter, removing a wooden spoon from the drawer. She turned the jet on beneath the pot, glancing back at him over the rumpled shoulder of her T-shirt.

"Chilly? There's a jacket behind the door."

He hadn't been inclined to say so, but once again she had read him without a need for words. He frowned and rose, moving to the hook she indicated to take down a faded sweatshirt jacket. Matt's? Why had she kept so many of his things?

He shoved his arms into the sleeves and jerked the zipper up before he sat back down. At the stove, she stirred the heating milk with one hand and put the other hand in the pocket of her holey sweats. The overhead light glinted in the sun-streaked highlights of her hair. Her shoulders hunched forward as if she, too, were chilled. Another jacket hung on a second hook, a smaller version of the one he now wore. He retrieved the garment and held it out to her. Without a word, she put it on.

This time he didn't sit down but turned his hips against the countertop and crossed his arms over his chest. "May I ask you something?"

She glanced up and away, but she didn't say no.

"Do you miss your husband?"

Ignoring him, she continued with the task at hand.

"Is that why you have his clothes still?" Caleb persisted, trying to understand. "To remind you of him?"

"I don't need that sort of reminder," she said, studying the steam rising from the pot. Judging the milk hot enough, she poured it into the mugs and flicked the burner off.

"Then why?"

Carrying both mugs to the table, she paused, pivoting on her heel. "I don't know. It's not exactly like I miss him. But I haven't wanted to get rid of anything of his. Call me a fool, if you need, but I'd like to know what makes you so certain that's not a normal course of events."

His mouth twisted at her tone. "I'm not entirely certain, which is why I'm asking. However, I've some inkling that people usually pack up the belongings of the…of people who aren't around anymore," he finished, crossing the linoleum to take his mug and sit down.

She pulled out the chair across from him, then lowered herself slowly to the seat. "Well," she murmured, "so they do." She said no more as she lifted the steaming mug to her mouth and drank. He drank, too, contemplating the curve of her lashes on her lowered lids.

After a moment, she placed her mug on the table. "How are you feeling?"

The color of her eyes reminded him of the horizon on a still, clear evening as the sun went down, the sky a blanket of velvet, the only light that brilliant line of green...

For the love of God, where the hell had that come from? Alarmed, he looked down at the table at the scratch of a word he still couldn't decipher. "Fine... Better, I mean. Not fine. I still can't remember anything."

She hooked the handle of her mug with her forefinger, moving the receptacle back and forth. "Caleb is a fine New Englander's name, but I don't think you're from around here."

"Why's that?" he asked, feeling a spark of something he recognized as dread.

"You don't have the accent. I don't either, so I recognize when it's missing. I'm from Pennsylvania originally."

"Pennsylvania," he echoed. The name meant nothing to him.

He watched her draw breath, take another sip, and set the mug back down. She tucked a handful of tangled hair behind her ear. "I looked in the phone book. And online. I couldn't find anything that would lead to revelations about who you are."

He nodded, not sure what she was talking about. The only thing clear to him was that she still had no idea who he might be or where he belonged. Lifting his mug, he drained the contents, scalding his tongue. "Ouch."

She smiled, a small turn of her lips. "You all right?"

"I'm all right," he said.

He wanted to touch her hand, her face, lean across the table and kiss her mouth, take his time, savor the sweetness of her lips and the residue of warm milk on her tongue. Instead, he stood up in a hurry and carried his empty mug to the sink.

"Matt used to do that," she said from the table.

Oh, God, he thought, remembering how clearly she read him. "Do what?" he asked, not turning around.

"Not wait for the milk to cool. He was always burning himself."

He let his breath out as he ran water into the heavy mug. When he spun back toward the table, she held her own close to her chin, staring off into middle space. Not wanting to intrude on her memories, he thanked her and left the kitchen to return to the guest room and his narrow, empty bed.

* * * *

Meg listened to the creak of the floorboards in the spare room above, followed by the slow groan of the bed frame. She lowered her mug to the table and stared down into the cooled remnants, the film of scalded milk shifting on top.

Yes, Matt used to do that before he climbed the stairs to shower or to bed, where he would wait for her to finish in the kitchen and join him. He would lean across the table and kiss her long and deeply in invitation while the flavor of warm milk was still shared in their mouths. Back when he still wanted her, when he'd leap up hard in anticipation of heated flesh, slick, private places, and the intoxication of abandon.

She let her breath out in a quiet sigh. Odd to find this stranger wanted to kiss her, too. Possibly, he possessed some psychic sensitivity of his own. Since he could bring forth no personal memories, he was perhaps more receptive to hers, reflecting them as if he and she were two mirrors held face to face, silvered surfaces casting back into infinity the image of the other until the origin could no longer be discerned.

After a moment, she got up to rinse her mug, then dried her fingers on the leg of her sweatpants. Turning out the light, she gazed through the window at the softly illuminated sea. She impatiently dismissed her theory as she recognized its distinct flaw.

Reflection would be impossible because nothing reflective existed in the darkness where she lived.

Exiting the kitchen, Meg headed to the living room, her destination before she'd heard Caleb descending the stairs. Some half-recalled sense of protectiveness had apparently urged him out of his bed to investigate. She was used to wandering around in the dark in her own home and hadn't given it a thought, but she really hadn't meant to startle him. Alarm couldn't be good for him in his condition.

The ambient light through the windows from outside bled the color from the carpet in the center of the hardwood floor. Deep shadows hid the identity of furnishings, but Meg knew every stick and its location by heart. She crossed with an unerring step to the hutch, a shade of gray–brown in the night. Opening the door, she gazed into the dark interior, the drawers hidden but for the dull gleam of the keyholes. What had led Caleb here? What errant thought of hers had entered his mind and made him curious?

She had watched him cross the floor as if drawn to the aged piece of furniture, saw him reach right out, open the door, and stare inside the way she did now. Rising up on her toes, Meg switched the three-way lamp on top of the hutch to its lowest setting. She pulled a key from the deep pocket of her sweatpants and inserted it into the top keyhole. As quietly as she could manage, she removed the drawer and took several steps backward to the sofa. Clutching the wooden receptacle in both hands, she sat.

Dog-eared birthday cards and Christmas cards, tattered notes and mementoes filled the drawer. The sum and substance of the good years with Matt. The years before he had changed and she with him. Before love had degraded and trust had altered. Before he had slipped into that bitter place where she refused to follow.

She tried to recall the first moment she had recognized the difference in their lives, but the change hadn't happened like that. She couldn't point her finger at a particular event and say, here is where the end began. It could have begun on the day they wed, really. At the exchange of vows when he became her husband and she his wife. *Until death do us part.*

Sometimes, though, it seemed death hadn't followed through with that promise. The scars of those final days, invisible to others, were always present in her mind. Though Matt had gone, the hurt remained like the sting of a phantom limb after removal. Even so, the pain had lessened of late. She had hoped, in time, to find it gone.

Meg frowned down at the box of fading memories. She should have chucked them all in the fire pit in the garden a long time ago. Hell, she should have taken an ax to the kitchen table, too. She told herself her practical nature prevented the latter. Not so. One day she'd hoped for an answer to the words he'd carved into the wooden surface.

So much for hope. So much for answers.

She gazed a moment longer at the drawer across her knees and then rose. Marching to the kitchen with it balanced against her hip, she paused only long enough to shove her feet into a pair of rubber boots and grab the box of matches before heading out into the night. Once there, she made her way to the garden. Meg dropped to her knees beside the fire pit and removed the lid. Grabbing a handful of items from the drawer, she hesitated briefly before spreading them over the metal bottom of the receptacle. Inhaling, she struck a match against the side of the box and set fire to the floral border of a card.

Meg watched the edges blacken and curl, flame moving across the decorated surface of the birthday card, consuming paper in a relentless crawl. She fed in another and then more of the drawer's contents, one item at a time, until nothing remained. Eyes surprisingly dry, Meg stood, the empty drawer dangling from her left hand against her thigh. Sparks drifted skyward, vivid against the darkness beyond until they faded to ash and disappeared.

She returned the mesh top to the pit and turned away. Somehow, she had expected to feel better about what she had done. Numbness tingled across her skin, touched her mind, and nothing more. Before going back inside, Meg glanced up at the ocean-facing windows of her bedroom, of the bedroom she and Matt once shared. Starlight shimmered across the glass surfaces, reflecting the velvet night sky.

In the nearest, a shadow moved and the curtain dropped back into place.

Chapter 4

Meg raced up the back stairs to the second floor in her unfastened rubber boots, stumbling at the top. She continued down the hall to her bedroom, and once inside, switched on the light.

The sash of the window where she thought she'd seen Caleb was raised several inches, the curtain fluttering slightly in a draft of air. Right. She'd forgotten she'd opened it. She really didn't believe Caleb would have wandered into her room, anyway, although if he had still been awake, he could have spotted the glow of the flames from the hallway and come to investigate.

Stepping back into the corridor, Meg listened. After a moment, she slipped out of the clumsy boots and strode toward the guest room. She paused outside the closed door. After turning the knob, Meg eased the door open and peered inside. Revealed in shadow and light, Caleb lay on his back, one arm flung above his head, jaw slack, mouth open with the growl of steady respiration passing in and out of his lungs.

Leaving the door slightly ajar, Meg returned to her room, the jolt of alarm fading, and in its place was a certain bemusement as she thought of Caleb asleep in his bed. It hadn't taken him long to slip back into slumber. Not surprising, considering his ordeal. She pictured the blankets twisted about his hips, his naked chest rising and falling with each breath. A beautifully made man, Caleb Hunter. She needed to forget that and sleep, too. The therapeutic effect of burning the drawer's contents should help. Yet, she didn't think it would.

Meg climbed into her bed and pulled the blankets to her chin as she stretched out on the sheet. Lying on her back, she watched the pattern of reflected starlight move across the ceiling for one hour, then into the next, listening to the sound of Caleb breathing across the hall where he slept soundly, cramped in the narrow iron bed. She told herself she had left his door ajar in order to hear him if he became restless or distressed. She told herself that as if it were true. Foolish, foolish, foolish, on so many levels.

What inhabited the night to change one's perspective? What was it about the closing of the day, the shadowed places, and the hushed quality of sound that made a difference? What, in the small hours of the morning, made loneliness more prevalent, made desire seem reasonable, made memory less bearable than the alternative…well, despite the pain memory brought. She wouldn't want to be in Caleb's position, without a past to recall.

Loneliness had become her companion, but not a pleasant one. Familiar, yes, comfortable, yes, but never comforting. Rolling onto her side, Meg punched the pillow with her fist several times before lowering her head back onto the cool surface.

The anniversary of Matt's death and she yearned for a stranger. A stranger she had dreamed about, but a stranger nonetheless. She had as little idea of whom and what he was as he did. Only a matter of a few hours old, the connection between them had no basis on anything practical or proven.

Sitting across from him at dinner, her eyes had strayed to his left hand. Usually, if a man wore a wedding band, some indication of its existence would show even if the ring of gold had gone, like an absence of tan line, a thinning of the flesh, a certain type of callous, something. But she detected none of those giveaways. The lack didn't preclude marriage, naturally, as he could have been one of those men who didn't wear a ring due to the hazards of his particular occupation. His hands certainly had the appearance of immoderate use.

What did he do for a living? At this point, who might be looking for him to return to his desk, his tractor, his ship? Could a child or children exist somewhere, a wife wondering what she had done to make him leave her, waiting in vain for him to walk in the door?

Meg closed her eyes, blotting out that picture. She knew he had no wife. Or she had at least become adept at convincing herself he had no wife, as the dark magic of the night constructed its web. With a snort of derision, she rolled to her other side, chiding herself for her weakness, her desperate loneliness on the anniversary of Matt's demise. She wanted comfort and physical closeness, and something about Caleb Hunter made her want *him* to fill that void. Maybe her good buddy, loneliness, had pushed her off the deep end.

But she knew better.

Damn it.

Settling herself, she listened to the sounds of the house. Wind rattled the glass and ruffled the chimes on the porch into musical annotation. Wood creaked, not from the pressure of a body's weight advancing across the planked floor—even though her mind had leaped to that conclusion in a heated rush—but from the contracting of cooling timbers in the weathered Victorian frame. In the front hall below, the grandfather clock ticked its metronomic rhythm. Hot water clicked through expanding pipes. Far from silent, yet the palpable emptiness of the house settled like a weight on her chest.

But it wasn't empty. It had never been. She was someone. And now there was another someone within its walls as well.

Someone with no memory of the specifics of his own life, but what did that matter? His injuries were not life threatening, no continued swelling, no headache, nausea, blurred vision, or slurred speech. He wanted somewhere safe for a time until he remembered things besides his name and that a person or persons had tried to kill him. He could be wrong about an attempt on his life, of course, given his battered recall. But if he wasn't wrong, then they might still be looking for him.

She should have considered that sooner.

Immobile beneath the quilt, she listened with renewed interest to the sounds she had identified only a few minutes earlier. Had she locked the doors? She rarely did. It would probably be a good idea to do so now.

Flipping back the covers, she stood up beside the bed, but she didn't turn on the light. Instead, she went to the window and parted the lightly blowing curtain. A chill draft fingered its way through the worn-thin fabric of her sweatpants. The isolated highway curving black in the night remained empty but for the glint of a car window beneath the stand of scrub pine up the road. A quick stop for teenagers bent on whatever teenagers did in the dark in their cars these days. Not much different from her youth, certainly. She moved to peer through one of the ocean-facing windows and pulled back the curtain. The garden below lay shadowed and whispering in the breeze. The beach showed no sign of habitation.

Biting her lip, Meg headed out into the hall and down the stairs, striding through the darkness to check the locks on the three doors and lower windows. In the room where she painted, she turned on the light, gazing at the illustration on the board, still unfinished. To the right, under the old sheet covering, rested the painting of the sea on its easel. She moved to stand in front of the easel and lifted the edge of color-smeared cloth to peer at a dark ocean that seemed to breathe with movement. Usually her own worst critic, she recognized the quality of the work. Even so, from her sudden detached perspective, she recognized the oppressive and deeply disturbing qualities of this particular painting.

It needed something to give it a little light. She had no idea of the time and didn't care as she squeezed paint from several tubes onto her pallet. With a few strokes, she painted an object into the foreground, well off-center so that it would not be the focus but an item of interest, and then proceeded to add detail, working quickly, filling in with color the object floating in the water, making the water wash over the bit of debris, the flotsam nearly concealed. Thrown up there, one might think, in the course of nature. She executed the object, following a stream of subconscious impulse. When she finished, she cleaned the brushes and returned to the painting. Looking at it, a chill coursed her spine.

She hadn't added just any bit of debris floating beneath the surface of the dark tide. Bobbing on the current, a broken board bore the name, nearly illegible, of her husband's ship: *Bonafide Venture*.

Stepping back, she pressed her hand to her mouth. "Oh, God," she whispered against the icy flesh of her palm.

What had made her do that? The addition had not elevated the subject matter but plunged the painting deeper into the darkness that had spawned it.

Backing away from the easel, Meg felt blindly for the light switch. Moving with speed through the shadowed house, she stumbled over a kitchen chair on her way to the stairwell. Shoving the chair back under the table, she limped up the steps to the guest room.

"Caleb."

He made a noise in his sleep but did not waken. Meg crossed the floor and lowered herself into the chair beside the bed, taking care the wood did not creak. She folded her hands between her knees. Turning her head, she stared through the window at the night sky.

The bedsprings groaned as Caleb rolled beneath the light cover. "What's wrong, Meg?"

He showed no surprise at finding her there, his tone sleepy, concerned. He sounded kind. Was he kind? She didn't even know that for certain.

"I'm afraid, Caleb," she said.

He didn't ask of what but reached out to take her hand in silence, closing his eyes and falling back asleep without letting go.

* * * *

Lying motionless on top of the blanket, Meg listened to the gentle, growling breaths Caleb made above her head, careful not to move, not to disturb him. She didn't want him to wake up and find she had crawled into the bed beside him. In subliminal recognition, he had known her there anyway, indicated by the fleeting, involuntary erection that rose and then receded against the curve of her posterior. Eventually his arm had come up as well, flopping across her waist. After, he had not moved, settling back into a deep slumber with his body pressed up against hers.

She found comfort in the closeness, even if stolen and premature and risky. She knew she took advantage of him, seeking solace and warmth where she had no right to expect any. But the contour of that single arm around her waist, the weight if nothing else, protected her. She, who prided herself on her independence and fortitude, recognized in the small hours of the night, lying beside a stranger, that it had been an outward show. Almost a defiance, as if somehow word would get to Matt she had survived his leaving her, continued in her career, made a life without him. Well, she had done all of those things and none of them, and now it didn't matter anyway.

Just let it go, she told herself. Just let it all go.

She had been telling herself that for three years, but it hadn't happened yet.

Suddenly Caleb's arm tightened around her. Meg's complacent acceptance of her own bold action—lying down beside a stranger—vanished with a thrust of concern. Caleb's hand moved under the hem of her shirt and settled around her breast, cupping the weight of it in an unconscious caress, perhaps in vague memory of another woman in his bed beside him. She didn't want to think on what that relationship might have been, might still be, once the details of his life returned to him. She didn't want to think at all, startled but aroused by a stranger's hand on her flesh. Holding her breath, she waited for his fingers to relax so she could pull them away without disturbing him.

They didn't relax. As she lay there, his thumb began to move across her stiffened nipple in slow strokes. She bit her lip to silence a verbal reaction to the sensation, of heat flooding her limbs, her loins, coursing through her blood. Her toes curled, her hips moved, and then she forced herself to lie still. He would stop. He would drift more deeply into slumber and stop. She would get out of his bed and return to her own. Hope he would have no recollection of what he had done to her in his sleep, so she would be able to face him in the morning.

But he didn't stop and she didn't get up. He took her nipple between his thumb and forefinger and began a gentle and erotic tug and release. Her heart thudded in her chest. The flesh between her legs grew slick. In a fiery instant of realization, she knew he no longer slept. He turned her onto her back as he rose up from the mattress beside her. Both hands pushed her oversized T-shirt up and over her head. She found herself exposed to the chill air, to the draft seeping in from the raised sash of the window, to the exploration of his hands over the stippled flesh of her breasts. His fingers moved across her stomach, then pushed the ragged sweats down over her hips. His fingers slipped between her legs, which parted willingly to his exploration as his teeth clamped lightly down on her nipple. She thrust her breasts eagerly toward him with a whispered word. *Please.* One hand in his hair and the other arm laced through the iron railing of the headboard, she arched her back further. Fired by her eagerness, Caleb greedily consumed her flesh with his mouth, seeking out and finding every nerve ending to increase her arousal, his fingers doing exquisite things to the flesh between her legs, stroking her clitoris until she was ready to explode. As his hands firmly grasped her thighs and his mouth closed over her, she arched up from the bed with a cry of release that echoed in her ears long after it had ended.

"Oh hell," she murmured, breathing hard, the word followed by one of his, not nearly as innocuous. He sat up, settling back over his heels. Her gaze darted to a discovery he slept in the nude. His erection stood firm against the line of dark hair trailing up his belly to the silky, curling mass on his chest.

The accusation in his eyes made her scramble up against the headboard, struggling into her shirt to hide her nakedness. "I'm sorry," she whispered, ashamed, swinging her legs over the side of the bed as she reached for her discarded sweatpants.

He closed his hand around her wrist. "Don't," he said. "Don't leave."

"I have to," she said.

"Please. Stay. Stay and talk to me."

At his tone, she wanted to weep. Instead, she shoved her legs into her pants and stood, yanking them up to her waist. Peripherally, she saw him watching as he moved to sit with his back against the headboard and pulled the blanket up to cover his hips. He remained hard, unfulfilled, but he seemed okay with that. He patted the mattress beside him.

"Sit," he said. "Talk."

Biting her lip, Meg slid back onto the mattress, tucking her bare feet under the sheet. Not so much for warmth but because she didn't want anything of nakedness between them. Of course, there was no getting around the fact he sat fully unclothed beside her. The only thing hiding his erection was the tented, lightweight blanket. The blood engorging his penis didn't look to be going anywhere else anytime soon. Meg turned her head away, drawing her knees up to her chest.

"I shouldn't have taken advantage of you like that, Caleb, climbing into your bed, looking for comfort, for...well, I wasn't exactly looking for what happened."

"I could have stopped," he said. "We both could have stopped."

"I know."

"It was nice. It was more than nice. You were...quick," he added delicately.

"Yes, well, three years alone will do that to you." If he wondered why she had been alone for three years when her husband had only been dead for one, he made no mention, perhaps too distracted to do the math.

"You didn't have any trouble recalling what you needed to do to make that happen," she said.

"I guess some things don't require conscious memory. Some things you don't forget."

"Like riding a bike," she murmured. He gave her a quizzical look from beneath his lashes but didn't ask. Meg let out a long breath. She listened as the wind picked up, causing a sudden, musical clamor on the porch.

"What is that?"

"Wind chimes," she explained. "Metal tubes of varying lengths are hung around a circular plate with fishing line, and when they strike each other in the wind, they make that noise. There are eight tubes, so they probably correlate to every note of a tonal octave. I don't know for certain. I'll show them to you tomorrow."

Beside her, he nodded, reaching over to take her hand. "What's this on your finger?" he asked, rubbing his nail along a bit of dried paint.

"I still couldn't sleep, so I was painting. I think I could sleep now, though," she admitted with a small laugh.

Without answering, he slid his hips down, pulling her close so her head lay on his chest. The folds of the blanket revealed his ebbing erection. She badly wanted to touch him, to stroke him back to eager hardness, but she kept her hand balled into a fist against the curling hairs of his chest.

"Go to sleep, then, Meg," he whispered above her head. "But tell me one thing first."

"What's that?"

"What were you afraid of?"

She opened her fingers into the soft, black curls on his chest. Beneath the drifting current of her steady respiration, his nipple stood erect. She knew what would happen if she touched him there, knew it as surely as if she'd already done so, as if she'd already explored the places that made him moan. Closing her eyes, she burrowed closer beneath the curve of his arm, breathing in his musky male scent.

"It might be easier if I told you what I wasn't afraid of," she said.

"All right," he agreed affably.

"You," she said. "I'm not afraid of you."

The rumble of a chuckle vibrated beneath her ear.

"And what we just did?"

"Not afraid of that either," she answered. His fingers moved through her hair, stroking the slightly damp locks back from her crown before they settled on her shoulder.

"I don't think there's much that frightens you, Meg Donovan, but there is something that does, and it seems to be undermining a great deal of your life. I'm glad it's not me. I'd like to do this again sometime."

She snorted in a distinctly unfeminine manner as she wrapped her arm around his waist. "Whatever you say," she murmured, leaving him to wonder to which of his three statements she'd responded. She closed her eyes again. Outside, the wind chimes continued their music, and she knew she would never hear them again without thinking of this night—this quirky, scary, perfect night. That was one of her problems. She attached meaning, significance, to everything, when sometimes none existed. Sometimes things happened. Period.

And sometimes, like with Caleb, the trail of significance in the wake of an occurrence stretched farther than she could hope to comprehend.

Chapter 5

Standing before the stone cross, Meg examined the plaque and names incised into brass. Matt was near the bottom, of course, listed with the three others who had gone down with him. Matthew James Donovan. Gary Martin Smith. Donald Sweetwater. James Jay Fitzhugh. She had known all but Donald, who had been newly hired for that fateful trip. Meg bowed her head out of respect for all of them, but her prayers were brief. Repose. Peace. She could ask no more than that for them now.

Beyond the cross and the circle of tarmac that wrapped around it, the little town stretched inland. The main street—which she viewed now—was a series of shops and businesses, whereas the lanes, radiating out from the main street in less than straight spokes, held late nineteenth and early twentieth century homes. Victorian frame houses, some in various stages of refurbishment, some falling into disrepair, dotted these streets with a few newer homes between. North of the "Point" stood the harbor and the fishery, the smell of both drifting down to the town when the wind was wrong. Today, however, the wind blew from the southeast and she could only smell clean sea air.

Watching the townspeople for a moment going about their business, she recalled the early days of her arrival. As insular as New England folk could be, they had accepted her right away. Perhaps because she had been Matt's sweetheart and Matt had been, at that time anyway, everybody's darling.

Glancing at her watch, Meg noted the hour getting on toward dinnertime. She needed to get the groceries in her car home. Still, she lingered, thinking of Caleb waiting for her there. She didn't regret her actions of the night before, not the white-hot velocity of the sexual act, not the fact she had fallen asleep in his arms, not even the fears that had driven her there. Her shame after they'd made love vanished in the gentleness of his embrace. Getting out of his bed in the pale light before dawn to return to hers had been a mistake. After the intimacy of the small hours of the night, waking up in separate beds had set the tone for the day. They moved shyly, almost awkwardly, through the morning's routines, and as the day progressed, so did the distance between them, a distance that should, by rights, have existed all along, but hadn't. It was all backward.

Even now, remembering the abandon with which she had welcomed his fevered attentions made her skin flush and her knees tremble. What on earth must he think of her?

With a canted, unclear frame of reference—if, indeed, he possessed any reference—would he see anything extraordinary about a woman who accepted a man she had just met under bizarre circumstances not only into her home, but also into her bed? Well, his bed. His loaner bed. Whoever's bed, her presence in it wouldn't go unremarked under normal conditions.

Of course, the conditions between them were not normal. They never would be. They had started out in peculiar fashion, bound to escalate once his recollection returned. The elements of their strange and accelerated relationship defied definition, goals, boundaries. The simple act of tending to a fellow human being in need had now been complicated by what she had let happen, what she had participated in, what she had precipitated by climbing into the bed beside him.

But would she go back and change it if she could? No.

Feeling her blush recede, Meg turned her back on the cross. Past her car parked at the curbside, the headland stretched out into the sea. Seabirds covered the promontory, massed along the rocky crest like snow. The spume from the waves fragmented into colorful prisms in the sun. Despite civilization, it remained a beautifully wild and rugged area. She understood why Matt had loved it so. She did, too.

Yet, upon raising her gaze to the endless appearance of the ocean, she shuddered. She could never share that particular affection. Never. The vastness of the ocean had always frightened her in some elemental fashion she could not explain.

"Meg!"

Yanked from her reverie, Meg observed the police car pull alongside her vehicle. The driver leaned out the window, arm crooked over the doorframe.

"Dan," she said, keeping the greeting carefully neutral. Stepping down off the curb, she crossed the empty street to stand a short distance from the driver-side door.

"Nice day," said the man who had brought her the news of Matt's death, who had grilled her for hours regarding Matt's activities before that, and then later, when it had become known Matt had moved out, paid her several impromptu visits on one excuse or another. Eventually, he had risked the frank disapproval of his superiors to ask her out. Though sufficiently good-looking to be the topic of frequent discussion in the female-oriented establishments around town, she wasn't interested. His wife had left him some years ago. Maybe he thought they had that in common.

"It is," she agreed. "A little chilly, but the sun is delightful."

He nodded, pushing his dark glasses up his forehead, his gaze moving openly in appraisal of her person. "You look different. Did you get your hair done?"

She sucked in her breath, feeling suddenly like a teenage girl walking into the house after a date with her sweater on inside out. The blush came roaring back.

"Dan, I can honestly say I've never gotten anything done to my hair that would make somebody stand up and take notice."

He continued to eye her with a peculiar expression. Perhaps he thought she blushed because of him.

"Well," he drawled after a moment, "you do look nice."

"Thanks," she answered.

He nodded again, a brief inclination of his head. The unit's radio crackled in static intrusion. He lifted the mike to provide a brief response. "Sorry," he said afterward.

"It's all right. You're working."

"I am," he responded, tapping his finger on the steering wheel. "Slow day."

"That's a good thing, isn't it?"

"Yup," he agreed and continued to idle his car beside hers.

Meg started to edge away, moving toward the back of the police unit. "I'll see you—"

"Nothing new up by you?" he interrupted, turning to look at her, his lazy smile dropping away. Yes, she remembered that expression and the way a seemingly innocent question held a deeper suspicion. Meg returning unwillingly to stand beside him again, trying not to let him see how he'd unnerved her.

"Not really," she stated, keeping her tone neutral.

"You've been shopping."

Noticing the angle of his head, she realized he could see the bags of groceries on her seat. "A person gets hungry."

"Sometimes a person needs a little company, too. Got enough in there for two?"

"As a matter of fact, I do. I'm expecting someone for dinner," she said, hoping to put an end to their conversation.

One sandy eyebrow lifted and then he nodded a third time, knowingly. "Good to hear, Meg. Anyone I might know?"

Did force of habit induce the guy to ask so many questions? Or was he trying to make a point? He couldn't possibly know she wasn't alone. For a moment, she was tempted to ask him what he hoped to accomplish with his interrogation but stopped herself. If he knew about Caleb, he would have said so straight out. That was his approach. He didn't often beat around the bush once he sunk his teeth into a morsel of knowledge, even when he had been trying to trip her up about Matt.

She shook her head in response, saying something about having company from out of town. He lowered his chin, sunglasses dropping down to settle low on the bridge of his nose. He peered at her over the frames through pale blue eyes. "Been seeing him a while, have you?"

Her eyebrows shot up. "No, I haven't."

He smiled. "Well, then, maybe you'll invite me up one night for dinner, too. I'll bring a bottle of something or other."

"A bottle of something or other?" she echoed, any inclination to be friendly vanishing altogether.

"Whatever you'd like. Wine. Schnapps. A little Scotch. Beer. Give me a call. You still have my cell number?"

"It's on your card." A card she had promptly thrown away. She hoped he wouldn't have the effrontery to ask her to recite it.

He didn't. Lifting two fingers in farewell, he began to ease the car along the street but quickly braked, jerking his chin in the direction of the stone cross. "Heard you were asking questions around town about any downed ships, any distress calls. Anniversary was sometime recent, wasn't it? Bound to get you brooding about that type of thing again. You get spooked out there by yourself, you give me a call. Five minutes. That's all it would take me to get to your place."

Meg couldn't quite figure out what to make of his offer. Still, he seemed to expect some kind of response from her. Any sort of gratitude expressed would only provide him an opening she had no desire to give him.

"If I need you, I'll call," she said.

Pale gaze direct, he nodded. "Promise?"

Meg sucked in a quick breath through her nose at his tone of challenge. With her own nod less in answer than dismissal, Meg walked around the rear of the patrol unit to her car. She opened the door, slid behind the wheel, and watched Dan Stauffer drive away. Nothing polite about the single-worded question, *promise?* Not the way he said it. He had been assertive, official rather than friendly, the way he had sounded when he had interrogated her, hoping to bully her into an admission of something she had no way of knowing.

But she *had* known. Or at least she had suspected Matt was involved in something he shouldn't have been. She had not cared for the position Matt had put her in, forced to be evasive when she'd been uncertain from what she needed to shield herself. She hadn't been willing to point fingers at shadows, wanting the truth from Matt first. In the end, he had neither admitted nor denied anything to her, and then he had gone.

Realizing she was in a similar position with Caleb, Meg turned the ignition key in agitation. Her interaction with Caleb, though, possessed one major difference. Caleb had not willfully withheld information from her. Whatever reason he possessed for avoiding the law had been shut away with his errant memory. Although she couldn't know for sure, she didn't believe he had done anything criminal. The sooner he remembered, the easier she would rest. Isolation could only last so long. Eventually something from the outside world would intrude and an altogether different sort of danger might arrive.

Chapter 6

Caleb sat on the low ottoman, his long legs at a sharp angle to his hips as he leaned forward, gazing at the instrument in his hand. He had a fairly good notion of its identity and use. After all, the cell phone in Meg's hand that first day had been familiar to him. But late this afternoon, he had identified with stark recognition the device's use when a series of numbers had popped into his head. For a good hour, he had carried the phone around, unable to make himself press the buttons coordinating to the numbers. He had no idea who he would be dialing. For all he knew, the number might belong to a killer.

Reaching up with his left hand to finger the still-sensitive knot beneath the tangle of his hair, he turned the phone in his right in contemplation. Any number of possibilities existed if he pushed the buttons, besides reaching the man who had tried to kill him. Failure to discover anything of significance might be one of them, raising more questions than answers. In another scenario, he imagined a woman answering the phone, a wife telling him of a life to which she rightfully expected him to return. The only woman that came to mind at this point was Meg. He held echoes of no others in his head. How would he deal with that? What if he never remembered anything or anyone else? Meg's presence had filtered into the blanks of his past, filling the barren niches with comfort and familiarity and now, after last night, a passion only briefly explored.

Drawing a deep breath, Caleb stretched out his leg and settled the phone onto his knee, then stared at the wall lost in thought. He remembered how she had climaxed in an explosion that had left her drained and, oddly enough, ashamed. He suspected his face had betrayed him when the thought had flashed into his mind, *how could you do this*? He didn't know where such a sentiment had come from or the flare of hurt, almost anger, accompanying it. But the damage had been done. Even if she hadn't witnessed the emotion in his face, she had sensed it, read it in the air between them in that odd way of hers. She did not deserve his bewildering reaction. He'd been quite happy she'd chosen to be with him in that fashion. He needed the closeness and so, it seemed, did she. If she hadn't been so withdrawn today, he would have talked with her about what had taken place between them, assured her in some way if he could.

Lifting the phone again, he tapped it several times on his kneecap before punching in the ten digits he had recalled. He brought the phone up to his ear. If he remembered correctly, he should hear a ringing, followed by someone speaking to him.

Instead, he heard a repeated and annoying tone. A busy signal. Yes. A busy signal. Hanging up, he tried again for no fewer than twenty attempts. Thwarted, he rose and strode out of the living room into the kitchen, where he set the phone in its cradle. Picking up a pencil, he wrote the number down on a piece of paper and shoved it in his pocket. In a while, he would repeat the process. Finding out anything would be better than nothing at all.

In frustration, he climbed the stairs to the second floor and walked down the hall to the bathroom to wash his face. Though the narrow room lay shadowed with the approach of evening, enough light entered for him to see what he needed to. Bending over the sink, he turned on the faucet and splashed his forehead, jaw, and mouth, then lifted his head to reach for the towel. An unfamiliar face looked back at him.

With a startled exclamation, Caleb spun around, hands raised in instinctive defense. Shadows ran long across the papered walls of the empty room. Shoving aside the shower curtain, he ducked swiftly to peer into the tub and then jerked backward. He glanced behind the door before darting out into the hallway, understanding, even as he did so, that no one could move that quickly. No one would be there. No one was.

For a long moment, he stood in the hall, listening to the sounds of the house, the waning day outside, while his racing heart steadied its pace. Turning around, he strode back into the bathroom and up to the splotched mirror. He half expected to find himself being watched by the face again, but the only countenance gazing back at him was his own.

"All right," he said aloud and then again, "All right."

Respiring evenly, deliberately, he examined the bruises that had come to the surface overnight on his jaw and throat. Abrasions marred his knuckles. His hands, wrists, and forearms were stiff and aching. He had put up quite the fight to prevent his own murder, and he was not a small man. The possibility he had struggled with more than one person seemed likely.

Oddly enough, that realization eased his worry. He hadn't been able to fathom what he might have done to make another man want to kill him. He'd feared the other man had acted in self-defense. But more than one man? No, an attack by multiple assailants would have been a deliberate and violent act that would have had nothing to do with any flaw or ruthlessness in his character. Right? That had to be right. He was a good, decent man. He wanted to be, anyway.

Leaning forward, Caleb tapped on the silvered, age-blackened glass with his finger. "Who are you?" he muttered.

His reflection wavered as the lighting in the room shimmered and changed. Dizzied, Caleb sat down on the closed toilet seat, one hand pressed to his roiling stomach. Damn it all. He didn't like feeling this way, sick and weak and disoriented. Something told him he had always been strong in the past, a man to take calculated risks, not stupid ones. A man in control. Not now. Oh, God, not now.

Hallucinations, or whatever one called sightings of faces not there, could not be a good sign either. He had to get better, he had to recall his life and what had happened to him most recently, who had tried to kill him and why. Not remembering formed a threat to both him and Meg. If the perpetrators learned he still lived, it would mean they had information about where Caleb had taken up temporary residence. Anyone could walk up to the door without Caleb's knowledge of their identity. If he wasn't alone when that happened, Meg would be in as much peril as he.

"Ah, hell," he said out loud. Meg didn't suffer from a knock on the head. Such an idea had probably already occurred to her. Last night, as a matter of fact.

Closing his eyes, Caleb lowered his brow onto his hand, riding out the wave of nausea. For the sake of Meg's safety, he should leave here, but where would he go? Since yesterday, this house, Meg's company, had become such a refuge from the uncertainty of his position that he could barely stand the thought of going away from her into the unknown. Any danger that might come to him here could follow him wherever he might wander, stalking him without identity, endangering anyone else who might endeavor to help him. Meg had suggested the police when he had first sought her help, and although he possessed only a rough knowledge of that organization, his aversion to their interference would not let him agree.

There was so much he didn't know and couldn't understand, causing him to react on a basic, instinctual level, and even instinct could be leading him astray.

With abrupt force, something clicked in his head, something fundamental to his personality. *Trust yourself.*

Rising slowly from his seated position, Caleb returned to the sink and washed his face again, then dried himself on the towel he had used that morning after he showered. He strode to the window and leaned against the sill. Pushing the curtain aside, he watched Meg's car pull into the driveway. She didn't get out immediately but sat behind the wheel studying the facade of the house. When she saw him in the window, she waved. He smiled.

Trust yourself.

Running his fingers through his damp hair, he went downstairs to help her with the grocery bags.

Chapter 7

Meg piled the dishes into the sink, running warm water and adding a dab of soap to let them soak. Watching the bubbles foam, she floated a moment in the intoxication caused by Caleb's nearness throughout dinner. She hadn't once given consideration to the concerns that had plagued her on the ride home. Even now, she dismissed them as soon as they suggested themselves to her again. Her whole being seemed suffused with warmth, disconnected and light as air, like a balloon with only a slim tether of ribbon to gravity.

"Meg, you okay?"

Caleb had come to lean against the counter beside her, heat and energy, hard muscle and warm blood, tendon and sinew and flesh. Solid. Grounded.

"Absolutely," she said.

He grunted in response, then nodded toward the sink. "Why don't you show me how you want those done?"

Meg's brows arched. "The dishes? They can wait."

"Show me," he repeated. "I'll learn fast."

Shrugging, Meg rolled up her sleeves and reached for the sponge. Caleb pivoted on his heel to stand directly behind her. She pressed a little closer to the sink.

"There's enough soap in here, but I like some extra directly on the sponge."

"Uh-huh," he said, an attentive student. Upending the bottle of dish detergent, Meg squirted lightly scented liquid onto the center of the sponge, squeezing the damp cellulose a few times to work up the lather. His hand closed around hers, imitating the movement of her fingers on the sponge before he eased it out of her grasp. "Let me."

She started to relinquish her position to him at the sink, but his other arm came down to her left and rested on the counter's edge. "Don't go away. Keep teaching."

The whole scene reminded her of one she had seen in a movie, and she wondered if the same film lurked somewhere in his subconscious. Dramatic and romantic, she remembered the outcome of that scene very well, and her tongue slipped out to moisten her lips.

Plunging her arm into the water, she brought out a plate, then slid her hand around the back of his, drawing it near to the dish. Foaming bubbles sluiced between her fingers and down her wrist. "You scrub the dish like this, or I do anyway, in circles."

He leaned his arms alongside hers as he followed her instruction.

"The water's quite warm," he commented. Suds, amniotic in temperature, ran in runnels through the dark hair on his forearms and over the downy blond hair on hers. His breath moved across her nape, stirring tendrils loosened from the clasp of her ponytail. She thought with fleeting intensity of the night before. Her pulse quickened.

"Can't get them clean without it." Turning the plate over, she had him repeat the process on the other side. "Set the dishes over there until we're ready to rinse them all."

He did as told, reaching into the water for the next item, performing the mechanics of the task with silent, superficial concentration, his mind, she suspected, not totally on the job. She turned her head to glance at him. He did likewise, smiling down at her with a closed curve of his mouth. She threw her thoughts at him in a fervent desire for him to kiss her, but it had never worked that way before. She couldn't make anyone do anything by thought process alone. She knew he got the signal, by her not-so-subtle body language more than any telepathic communication, when he smiled again, bending closer.

"This is enjoyable," he whispered near her mouth, then straightened and resumed his undertaking.

Her right knee jerked and struck the cabinet door.

His firm chest pressed close, the thudding of his heart beneath the surface of his flesh vibrating over the curve of her spine. She watched the newly familiar shape of his arms from beneath her lashes as he squeezed excess soap from the sponge, the tendons in his wrist standing up, the muscles of his forearm tightening before release. Foam splattered her face and the neckline of her tank top beneath her open collar, water running down over the swell of her breast and into her bra in a warm, slow trail.

"Sorry," he apologized softly.

"Not a problem," she assured him.

He continued to wash and she continued to watch, fascinated by the confident action of his hands, the knowledge of his body close to hers, the humming vibration of his energy in the narrow space between them. He confined his activity to dishwashing, but a sultry promise guided every move he made. It seemed to her he didn't merely lave a dish, the interior of a glass, or the length of a knife, but demonstrated a technique of motion that when transferred at last to her body would cause her to lose all restraint. She could barely keep from squirming where she stood or slipping out from beneath his arms to stand safely on the other side of the kitchen.

As he neared the end of his task, searching out the last of the items in the water, he began to hum a tune above her head. She listened, recognizing with a start the refrain to an old Van Morrison tune. Obviously, a bit of memory had seeped through. Leaning forward, Meg drained the sink, humming along with a smile. She turned on the water to rinse the dishes and stack them in the drainboard. As soon as the last one had been set in place, Caleb reached past her to turn off the water. He pulled her away from the counter, his wet hands on her shoulders before sliding down to her waist. She lifted her face to him uncertainly. With a laugh, he clutched her fingers and began to lead her in a slow dance around the kitchen floor to the tune vibrating from his chest.

He held her close, the dampness seeping from his hands through her clothes. It took her a moment to realize the rumbling song from his unclear recollection had ended and he held her in silence, rocking slowly in the middle of the floor, his unshaven jaw turned against the top of her head.

"Are you remembering something?" she whispered.

"No," he answered, but his voice held a note of strain. She pulled away to look at him for the truth behind the word, but then he kissed her.

Startled, she sucked in her breath, sucked in the warm air of his lungs, and opened her mouth to meet the gentle exploration of his tongue, her thoughts of protest spinning away, her arms clinging across his back and neck to keep herself grounded. His body pressed nearer, heated and lean and hard, while hers seemed to lose all solid consistency. He held her tighter, one hand in the small of her back, pulling her close against his hips where he strained erect in the confines of his borrowed jeans. His other hand opened along her throat, fingers pressed to the battering pulse beneath her jaw. Curling her fingers into the fabric of his shirt, she drew him backward across the floor until they were once more against the cabinets.

He pulled his head away slightly, looking a question into her eyes.

"Don't stop kissing me," she said. "Don't stop anything."

With his mouth on her own, he lifted her onto the countertop. His hands moved beneath her blouse, easing her bra straps down into her sleeves. He slid his thumbs along the curve of her collarbone, then down into the soft cup of her undergarment to tease her nipples until they stood erect against his fingertips. Pressing his forehead against hers, he whispered, "May I take this off?"

"My bra?"

"All of it."

She nodded against him and found herself quickly naked from the waist up, her clothes in a heap beside her on the counter. He cupped her chilled breasts in his palms. She looked down at the contrast of his tanned fingers against the creamy hue of her skin, her nipples taut in yearning. Bending from the waist, he took first one into his mouth, then moved to the other, pulling with the edge of his teeth. The damp residue from his tongue chilled in the air across each tip. Eagerly, she thrust her breasts toward him, wanting more, the delicacy of his touch exquisite.

With his hands around her rib cage, he repeated his action, not once but many times, until Meg found her breath coming fast and shallow. Heat shimmered across her skin and flooded into her abdomen.

From the sound emanating low in his throat, Caleb understood her urgency, possessed a similar one of his own. He tugged her hips toward his as his head came up, his mouth fastening hard on hers. She wrapped her legs around his waist, the back of her head bouncing without pain against the cabinet behind as he drove against her, speaking her name into the hollow of her mouth. His hips pushed into the curve of her thighs, his erection driving the seam of her trousers against the soaked cotton of her panties. She moaned and tightened her arms around his neck as they rocked together, thwarted by layers of fabric. She came, hard and long, shuddering and wrapped in his embrace. He whispered against her face, her throat, the swell of her breasts, gentle words of intimacy. She savored the familiar cadence of his endearments, the rush of voice and breath across her skin.

Lifting her from the counter with her legs still around his waist, he headed for the stairs. At the base, he paused.

"Don't carry me up, Caleb. I'm too heavy."

"You don't weigh a thing," he whispered, setting his foot on the first step.

She shook her head, struggling free of his arms to stand on the step above, her height on level with his. He lowered his foot back down beside the other, hazel eyes moving warmly over her flushed breasts. Lifting a hand, he encircled one, rubbing his thumb across her nipple. The heat began anew, simmering in her flesh. With his other hand, he unfastened the button of her pants and slowly pulled down the zipper. He released her breast to push her pants down her legs. She stepped out of them.

Hooking the edge of her panties, he pulled them aside and slid the fingers of his other hand along the soaked contours of revealed flesh. He dropped down onto his knees.

"Oh, God," she breathed.

He laughed, a low sound, less of amusement than pleasure. When he opened his mouth over her, his tongue moved in slow, sultry, sensual demand. Her knees trembled. She clutched the banister for support, finding she had no breath, no voice, no cognizance but that of the place where his tongue circled lazily, urging her in delicious increments toward climax. His hands on her thighs, he pushed her down onto the step, and then his mouth held her there, trembling in captivity as he unfastened his jeans. He slid them to his knees.

"Caleb," she whispered.

The utterance of his name seemed to galvanize him, the moment hanging suspended in a glittering, crystal instant. Straightening his spine, he took the pressure of her weight off the wooden step with his hands as he slid the engorged length of his penis inside of her. She barely recognized the sound escaping her throat.

She arched her back against the rounded edge of the step, sheering away from her isolating loneliness into the curl of pure sensation as he thrust between her thighs. He filled her completely, his hands protecting her from the full impact of his driving need. The texture of his tongue coursed over hers, the flavor of his mouth sweet and heady. Groaning, he pulled out of her, some buried retention of precaution causing him to shudder in completion against her thighs. After, he held her close, breathing heavily into her hair.

"Sweetheart," he whispered, "don't cry."

Only then did she realize the nature of the dampness on her cheeks.

"Oh, Caleb," she whispered, scrubbing the tears with the back of her hand. "I don't know why I'm crying. I'm sorry."

"Shh." He pulled away, smiling down at her before making a face at the condition of her underwear. "I think you need a shower."

"Yep," she agreed.

"Are you okay?"

"I'm fine."

She wasn't, not entirely, but he didn't need to know. Although she'd had sex with a stranger, a fact that both appalled and exhilarated her, she also knew Caleb was not a stranger at all. Some part of her knew him, recognized him, remembered him in a manner she could not explain. For the space of several drawn breaths, she studied the eyes gazing back into her own. She kissed him gently on the mouth.

"Are you joining me?" she asked as she struggled, rubber-legged, to her feet.

"I'm going to step outside for a bit of air and then I'll be up," he said, reaching for his jeans. Meg bit her lip. Was he aware of the strangeness, too?

She knew he was, as surely as if he'd said the words aloud.

Chapter 8

Dan Stauffer lowered his binoculars against his thigh, digging with his other hand in the pocket of his coat for his cigarettes, then remembering after a few fumbled attempts that he had given up that particular vice some months ago. Bad timing, that. He could have used one about now.

Leaning back in the seat, he stared through the car window at the house, white faded to gray in the night, the lights on downstairs in the kitchen. For the past three years, his irregular vigils had always shown it to be the same. A light burning in one room or another defined Meg's nightly routine, until the final lamp in her bedroom upstairs. Sometimes it stayed lit until the wee hours, and sometimes it shut off within minutes. Tonight, however, had been different. Tonight, she had not been alone.

Hell, how much of a friggin' pervert was he, watching, but once they had begun, he hadn't been able to turn away. He'd always known there was something about her. Meg Donovan had a look. She drew men's eyes without knowing it, by the way she walked, her quick laugh, her firm and vigorous female shape. Tonight, he'd seen a great deal more of her than he had ever hoped to witness. She had breasts that could stop a man's heart in his chest, and that guy she was with had enjoyed every inch of them for a good, long time.

Dan released a shaking breath, shifting his hips in an attempt to relieve the uncomfortable restriction in his trousers. Stretching across to the glove compartment, he flipped it open, not too concerned about the tiny light showing. Meg's place stood in an isolated location, and he figured neither one of the two occupants would be glancing out the window anytime soon. Whatever was taking place in their grand finale had moved out of his viewing area, but he had a healthy imagination and didn't need the binoculars to tell him what they were doing now.

Grabbing an open pack of gum, Dan shut the compartment and slid the paper off the end of a stick, drawing it into his mouth with his teeth, then leaned back into the seat again, the spice of cinnamon burning pleasantly on his tongue. Pressing the curve of his close-shaven skull against the cloth headrest, he closed his eyes, trying hard not to let his imagination get the best of him. He had always hoped, despite his investigation, that he would be the one with whom Megan Donovan broke her extended solitude. He had spent more than a few sleepless nights in covetous contemplation of such a coupling. A woman like her, alone for so long, was bound to be hot for a stiff cock. What he had glimpsed taking place on the counter through the kitchen window had been proof positive of that.

It had been a year since the *Bonafide Venture* had gone down and three years since Matt Donovan had walked out of his wife's life. She deserved a little fun, even a new relationship, although from what he glimpsed of this guy, he didn't look familiar, not anyone from around here, so Dan couldn't be sure what the heck would come of it. Maybe she'd give up the house and move to wherever this guy came from, but he doubted it. She'd grown up in Pennsylvania and hadn't shown any inclination to move back there yet. He didn't think she wanted to leave. Uncommonly attached to the place, all things considered. Like she was waiting for something.

And what, he mused, eyes still closed, might that be? He had to stop being so suspicious. His nature prodded him to constantly question motives, and considering what he had learned of Matt's activities early on, it had seemed unlikely to him that Meg had no knowledge of her husband's illicit pastimes. As time went by, he had reconsidered that notion. Matt was careful, didn't leave any loose ends. There'd been talk about him moving his operation to the Caribbean. He might have managed that, too, if the storm hadn't taken him and the other three down into the ocean.

As for Meg's reasons for staying despite the hurt, the humiliation, well, she did have a life here. She had a few close friends, a looser circle of association, a career, the house. That piece of prime real estate had risen in value over the past couple of years. With a little cosmetic sprucing, she could sell it for a bundle and move on. However, he had come to realize that Meg liked where she lived. She liked the architecture and history of the house, the isolation of its position, the nearness of the beach, the waves. She wasn't particularly fond of the ocean itself, though. No surprise there.

If she had any clue how much she'd unintentionally revealed to him, she wouldn't be thrilled. She didn't care for him much, he could tell. But occasionally she talked to him, and he was always listening.

Opening his eyes, he noticed the porch light had come on. He couldn't see the back porch directly, only the nearest end of it. The glow of the wall sconce along the length of the railing and in the landscaped grasses created a pale nimbus of illumination in the gathering mist. A shadow passed through the light and leaned against the railing. Him. The Guy.

They had been quick after all. No afterglow cuddling session? Curious, and a little envious, Dan raised the binoculars again.

The guy didn't have a shirt on, only a pair of jeans in the chilly night. Still, he didn't huddle into himself in protection against the chill but stood staring out into the darkness. Despite his stance, Dan could see he stood loose-limbed, relaxed, obviously sated. A twinge of—what? Jealousy?—shot through him. But when the fellow turned his head into the light, his expression revealed an attitude contrary to his appearance. Dan sat up.

The guy's eyes looked cold. Hard. Calculating. Or at least they seemed to. At that distance, it was difficult to tell. A moment later the man's expression changed, softened, a smile curving his mouth, and an instant later again became hard. Dan watched as Meg's lover raised a hand to his head as if it hurt, then lowered that same hand back down to the railing. The man tilted his chin up, turning his head, his shoulders, his whole body, until he appeared to be looking directly at Dan across five hundred feet of night-driven darkness.

Swearing aloud, Dan held himself immobile, waiting. There was no way—*no way*—this guy could see him, not even the glint of his binoculars. Parked off the road beneath the blowing shadow of a stand of wind-bitten pines, the car should have been invisible. He'd been there countless times before without even a glance from passing motorists. Still, the dark haired man on the porch continued to gaze in his direction, looking for all the world as though he stared straight into Dan's eyes through the circle of the binocular lenses. The fine hairs on Dan's neck shifted. The dashboard clock flashed from one minute into the next before lover boy finally looked away. Dan released his breath.

Hell, that had been an odd sensation. Reaching up, he smoothed the hair down at the back of his neck. After a few minutes, the fellow walked out of sight, and the porch light went out. Dan shifted the binoculars' focus and found the guy striding through the kitchen. In another minute, that light went out also, leaving only a single window illuminated upstairs. The bathroom?

The clock read 9:08. He'd wait a bit more. Something down by the water before darkness fell had caught his interest. He had no idea what it might be, but his eye had been drawn repeatedly in that direction while the light had lasted. Curiosity burned through him. He couldn't explain why, but now that their dance in the kitchen had ended, the desire to sneak down to the beach and check it out overwhelmed him. After he had a look, he would call it quits and go home. His surveillance was unofficial. If he ever got caught now the investigation had been closed, he'd be without a job. So he waited a quarter of an hour until the light in the bathroom went out before he reached under the seat for his flashlight.

Opening the car door, Dan stepped out onto sparse vegetation after taking the precaution of turning off the interior overhead light. He listened a moment before closing the door without noise, the latch barely secured. He crossed the street at the far side of the weathered fence that bordered one side of the property. By daylight, the thinly built barrier would provide no protection from eyes that might seek him out, but under cover of night, he would be nothing more than another shadow.

At a distance, he passed the porch and looked that way, finding it empty. Last night, Meg had been burning something in the wee hours. He had seen the glow of a small fire from his car parked beneath the trees. Perhaps she and the boyfriend had been having a snog session around that fancy fire pit of hers.

Stepping out onto the beach below the end of the fence line, loose sand shifted beneath his sneakers. The foam of the surf looked luminous in the black curl of the breakers. With the occasional glance at the house, he headed toward the water's edge, walking slowly, hiding the beam of the flashlight against his thigh, flicking the switch on and off to illuminate the damp sand. He spotlighted seaweed, debris, shells, pebbles, the occasional bit of trash…

"Holy Mother of God," he whispered.

For the second time in a matter of minutes, the short hairs rose at his nape. What were the chances of this occurring? Squatting, he shone the torch beam along a surface of roughened paint. Christ, last time he had seen this thing, it had been hanging in the cabin of Matt Donovan's fishing boat the day before he made that final trip. The deterioration didn't correspond to what an object should look like after spending a year in salt water. He frowned, bending closer.

Something didn't make sense. Something didn't make sense at all.

Fingerprints weren't going to matter at this point, even if he could gather any. Even so, he slipped the end of his jacket sleeve down to cover his hand as he grasped a corner of wood. Flicking off the flashlight, he stood up in the darkness. His unease persisted. Feeling watched, he glanced to his right and to his left, then over his shoulder toward the house. Not far from his feet, the dark tide purled against the shore, the sound of driven and receding water rhythmic and pervasive.

The currents had a prevailing pattern. It was what made maritime navigation such a tricky business for the novice seafarer. And the *Bonafide Venture* had gone down to the northeast and fourteen nautical miles out to sea. He would need to check his facts, but he was fairly certain what he held in his hand would turn out to be a physical impossibility.

Suddenly anxious to be on his way, Dan headed back in the direction he had come. It wasn't long before he became aware of footsteps dogging his own. He couldn't tell how far away or from where they originated, but they kept perfect time with his pace, crunching through the sliding sand. Halting abruptly, Dan spun around, clutching the battered wood against his chest. No one there.

With an expulsion of air from his lungs, Dan pivoted around on his heel. Dread, unexplainable and unnerving, crept over his skin. As he made his way across the sand toward the looming fence line, a shadow formed from the starlit night, blocking his path.

Chapter 9

Meg sat on the edge of the mattress, the only illumination in the room the night-light in the base of the bedside lamp. When she'd come out of the bathroom, she'd found the lights off downstairs, but Caleb had not joined her in the bathroom, nor did she find him in his bed. She wondered where he had gone. Would he have set off for a stroll on the beach at night? It didn't seem likely. She only hoped nothing in their recent activity had resulted in renewed physical distress. She couldn't see why it would, but the thought of it caused her to get off the bed and slip a pair of jeans on beneath her T-shirt. Feeling around with her toes beneath the edge of the nightstand for her flip-flops, she turned her head at a noise in the doorway.

"Caleb," she breathed.

He looked upset. Given the state of his fractured memory, there could have been any number of things troubling him but only one came to mind.

"Are you sorry that we—?"

Shaking his head, he stepped into the room. When he smiled at her, a curve of his mouth and no more, the light touched his eyes. Relieved, she went to him, stopping an arm's length away. She reached out and slipped her finger into the loose curl of his fist against his thigh. Sand salted the carpet by his bare feet.

"I'll never be sorry we did that," he said, pulling her close to press his mouth to her hair. "Never."

"Not even if you remember there's someone else waiting for you somewhere?"

"Shh."

A tremor shifted the flesh of his thigh against the back of her hand. She tightened her hold on his fingers. "I don't know what we do now," she whispered. "Making love with you wasn't wrong, but there's no history between us and no future to be foreseen. Do you lie down beside me, or do we sleep alone in separate beds? Do we behave as if this hasn't happened between us or continue in the path we've chosen tonight? I don't know what we do now," she repeated.

"We take comfort in the moment," he said quietly, "and wait."

"For what?"

He made a noise, an expulsion of air through his nose that was no answer, sounding more like a dismissal of the topic.

"Come to bed, then," she said, leading him by the hand. He hesitated, holding her back before following. At the foot of her bed, he unzipped his jeans, lowered them to the floor, and stepped out of them. A mist of fine sand sprayed from the hem.

"Maybe I should shower first," he suggested, frowning down at his feet.

"Just brush them off. I'll run the vacuum tomorrow."

He did so as she pulled down the quilt and slipped out of her own pants. Once he had climbed into bed, she turned off the light. It occurred to her, as she stood blinking for a moment in the sudden blackness, that she should be afraid or, at the very least, apprehensive of trusting a stranger to such a degree she would lie beside him and sleep. But she'd done it once already and had derived a great deal of comfort. She wouldn't question. She would let it be.

"I don't know who I am. I don't know what I am," he said as she climbed beneath the blankets. His words chilled her.

"Sometimes it feels like the past is battling in my head. Like I can hear it calling to me in a voice I don't recognize, but it doesn't come out of hiding, and I'm afraid that's because it can't. Meg, I wish you could tell me one thing about me. One thing, so I wouldn't have to fear the man I might truly be."

Meg bit her lip. In the darkened room, propped on her elbow, she searched his face, his eyes, for some hint of what he needed from her to no avail. Lying on his back, breathing steadily and deeply, he waited for her response. Meg found no shimmering thoughts she could snatch from the air now. She closed her eyes.

"It seems to me," she began, "that you are a kind man, and patient. Soft-spoken but not timid." Lifting her lids, she took his hand, turning it over. "Your palms are calloused. You've worked hard. You're strong—you appear capable. Whoever did this to you"—she reached up to touch her fingertips to the bruises on his throat and lower jaw—"probably caught you off guard. I don't think you're the type to let that happen a second time."

Briefly, she envisioned the act, the violent impulse, the flurry of punches, the curled fingers seeking to choke the breath from his lungs, the desperate struggle, man against man, perhaps more than one man, the image so strong she found herself flinching, and she knew then what she visualized was truth. She swallowed, trying to calm her racing heart rate. Only Caleb's face was clear to her in the blur of motion.

Beside her, Caleb shook his head negligibly. "If that person walked up to your door tonight, I wouldn't know who the hell he was," he said, his agitation tempered by pressing his lips against the pulse in her wrist. She stared in a moment of contemplation at the place where his mouth had been.

"That's true enough," she said. "But the doors are locked, and I know the only visitors I ever get. Besides you, that is. So, we'll figure if I don't recognize them, they're suspect. How's that?" She wondered how long he had been worrying about this. She had thought to keep that concern from him, but apparently there had been no need. He had worked it out, same as she had.

He relaxed as she touched the lines beside his eyes, alongside his mouth, ran a finger lightly along his lower lip. The dark stubble of his jaw rasped beneath the heel of her palm.

"You've laughed a lot. Squinted in the sun. You run your fingers through your hair when you're troubled," she added, realizing how many times she had seen him do that. "Should I go on?"

"Could you?" he asked in a dubious tone.

"Your hair could use a trim," she said, tugging gently on a lock. "I'll do that for you if you'd like."

His lips twisted in a crooked smile. "I'd like."

"And I'll shave you, too." She rubbed a digit across the dark shadow of his jaw.

"Sounds sexy."

"It certainly could be."

Snatching her hand, he turned her palm against his mouth. She closed her eyes as warmth rushed into her veins. She had never been the type to kiss a man until she knew him fairly well and had never picked up a stranger in a bar and taken him home for the night, ever. So what had changed in her? What enabled her not only to accept what he offered, but also welcome it, invite it, revel in it, despite the circumstances that had thrown them together?

"Caleb," she said, "when you remember your life, you might not think much of me."

"Don't be ridiculous," he murmured into the curve of her palm before he yanked her on top of him, hard again against her belly. She pushed up from him so she could look down into his face. Her hair brushed across his naked chest, mingling with the dark, silky hairs curling out of his skin.

"In certain circles, the fact that I had sex with you when we only met yesterday wouldn't speak very highly of my moral character. But I promise you, it's not something I've done before."

"What? Had sex? I doubt that."

His hands wriggled her shirt up past her waist. One arm settled across the small of her back while the other hand continued to maneuver the cloth over her head. She pulled her head out, allowing him to free both of her arms and toss the garment aside. Her breasts settled against the warmth of his chest.

"That's not what I meant. I don't know you—"

"But you do," he interrupted. "You revealed quite a bit about me. Knowledge starts with little things and then grows."

"Sort of like this?" she asked, closing her hand around him and laughing.

Before she could draw another breath, he had flipped her over onto her back and sprawled across her, effectively pinning her to the mattress. Fitting a knee between her thighs, he wriggled them apart, settling himself in between.

"I like that you're playful," he said, kissing her chin as he wrestled her wrists into one of his hands. "I always have," he added, reaching down to touch her between the legs. At his words, she stilled, gazing into his eyes in the darkness. Confusion showed fleetingly on his face as he stared back at her.

"It's a jumble," he said. "I think I remember something, and it ends up I couldn't possibly. You're all that's familiar to me right now." Lowering his weight over her body, he held himself up on his elbows. Pressing against her, he slipped inside with a single thrust. Her vaginal muscles convulsed around him. He sucked in his breath, looking down at her with a smile in his eyes.

"I need you desperately," he said, "and I believe you need me. Let's just leave it at that for now."

* * * *

She slept with her back to him, her head heavy in slumber on his outstretched arm, her honey-gold hair soft against his skin. Caleb stared at the ceiling. He would have given anything—well, just about anything— to remember. Not only to remember who he was, where he was from, what his life had been, but to know, truly know, why Meg Donovan was in his life now. There had to be a reason. He knew there had to be a reason, though he couldn't fathom what it might be.

He listened to the sounds of the house, recognizing each as the same he'd identified the night before. Nothing unusual there, nothing suspect. They were safe, or relatively safe. He should sleep. But he couldn't.

Because he couldn't remember, he tried to work out what had happened in a logical fashion. Someone had tried to kill him. Okay. Where had this taken place? Not here on the beach. There had been no evidence of a struggle around where he had awakened. Besides, he was certain Meg would have been aware of any commotion from the execution of such an act. Also, if the struggle had taken place on the beach, he would probably still have his clothes. If he had been dropped there, he could have been stripped of his clothing to mask his identity in some way. But there had been no sign of him having been dragged across the sand. He must have come up on the beach from the water. If he had been thrown from a ship, or fallen overboard, he could have washed up with the tide. That being the case, the chances that anyone would know where he had landed were probably slim. Wouldn't that mean he and Meg shouldn't have to worry the person who had tried to do him in would come after him here in her home? Still, he wasn't willing to relax his vigil altogether based on that vague supposition. He could have wandered nude along the shoreline for a distance before collapsing, and the scene of the attempted crime might be right beyond the jetty of jagged black rock.

Gently removing his arm from beneath Meg's head, he stretched the tingling limb while pulling the blanket up over her shoulder with his other hand. Her skin shone in the night with a pearly luminescence. Lowering the quilt into place, he tucked the edges close. He fingered the soft strands of her hair. "Meg," he whispered, easing himself off the mattress to stand in the darkness beside her bed.

She slept on, undisturbed. He watched her for several seconds before walking around the foot to the window, where he slid the curtains aside on the rod. He leaned his forearm against the sash and his brow against the cool glass, gazing out into the night. A distance away across the dulled, black ribbon of winding roadway grew a stand of trees, their shadows grossly misshapen, weather-beaten. He found his eyes drawn there, fixed on the blackness beneath the trees. His heart rate quickened, thudding in his chest.

Earlier tonight when he'd stood out on the porch, he had…sensed? Was that the word? Yes, sensed something there. Or someone. Like a dream half remembered, it all seemed rather vague. And he knew what dreams were because he had dreamed last night while he slept, waking to find he couldn't bring the fleeting images back for total recall. His unclear recollection of those few moments on the porch disturbed him. Closing his eyes, he strained to picture it again. While leaning against the porch railing, he had imagined himself out on the beach. As for what he had envisioned occurring there, the imagery came to him in abstract fashion. No matter how hard he tried, he couldn't collect enough pieces of his elusive trek into the sand to fit them into a whole. The entirety of the event had been like some nightmare, even though he hadn't been asleep. Remembering what the doctor had said about internal bleeding, he reached up and cupped his hand over the back of his head.

The tenderness had nearly gone, the swelling no more than an annoying bump. He didn't believe his hallucination had been caused by his injury. But what, then?

Frustrated, he sighed, clouding the glass with his breath. He turned away from the window and moved across the room, allowing his galloping heart to calm.

He couldn't tell Meg what he had experienced because she would insist he seek treatment at a hospital. But treatment wouldn't make a difference. Whatever was taking place inside of him, in his body, in his head, would remain unexplained, would be a source of curiosity, of endless questioning, probing, and in the end, the result would be the same. There would be no answers. He would never again be who he had been.

Be who he had been, not *know* who he had been. A big difference between the two. Why did his thoughts go there? Frowning, he turned again to look at Meg in the bed, listening for a moment to her soft breathing. His hands clenched into fists on his thighs to keep them from shaking. He wanted to wake her, take comfort in her body, in their closeness, but he spun away, disgusted with himself, with his weakness.

Searching the floor for his jeans—for Matt's jeans, he corrected himself—he found them by the footboard and shimmied into them. In the bed, Meg spoke in her sleep, a single unintelligible word, and rolled onto her back but did not waken. The blanket slipped down to reveal the rounded swell of the tops of her breasts, milky white in the gloom. Caleb left the room. In the hallway, he paused on the worn runner, shoving both hands into his pockets. His fingers touched a folded piece of paper.

What better time than the middle of the night to reach someone? When people—untroubled people—should be in bed asleep? It could be worth a shot. If he woke up the owner of this number, fine. He would face whatever he had to. If they chose not to answer or slept through the call, at least he had tried again.

Walking softly, he made his way down to the kitchen, pausing at each creak of the stair treads. Turning the light on over the stove, Caleb took the phone from the wall and sat in the chair at the table's head, cradling the instrument in his hand on the tabletop. His gaze shifted to a place beyond where he had seen the scratching of a word in the surface his first day here—was that only yesterday? He didn't see it now, but he suspected the damage might be concealed by the newspapers Meg had dropped there earlier. She said she planned to put them out for recycling. He wondered now if she'd left the folded papers on that spot purposefully. Perhaps she considered whatever was written there to be none of his business. And she'd be right.

In the front entryway, a tall clock, what Meg had referred to as a grandfather clock, counted time with a deep, monotonous tone. Caleb didn't bother to turn around and look at the smaller face of the round clock hanging on the kitchen wall. Meg had spent a few minutes going over the mechanics of telling time with him before dinner, but he didn't quite see the necessity in testing himself. The hour was somewhere between sundown and sunup, and that was enough.

He took several long breaths, readying himself. Holding the phone in one hand and the piece of paper in the other, he pressed the numbers with the pad of his thumb. Lifting the receiver to his ear, he waited, only to be met by the same repetitive signal he had earlier. What did that mean? Swearing beneath his breath, he repeated the process.

"What are you doing?"

He jumped, swiveling on the chair to look at Meg in the shadowed stairwell. She blinked at him, sleepy-eyed, her honey hair tousled around her face. She wore the T-shirt he had removed and nothing else.

"What are you doing?" she asked again with a note of suspicion. She stepped down into the kitchen and crossed the floor. Standing beside him, she stared hard at the phone and then at him, her expression troubled.

"I…I remembered something earlier today. I remembered what this thing is," he said, waving the phone with the dull tone still repeating itself hollowly in the air, "and I remembered a number. A series of numbers, to be more precise, and I dialed them. All I get is this beeping noise, though."

What did she think? That he had been lying to her about his memory loss, secretly making calls in the middle of the night? Actually, if she thought that, he couldn't blame her. But he didn't know how to explain himself without sounding like he was trying to convince her he hadn't been lying. Instead, he handed the phone to her. She took it in a fierce grip, fingers curled tightly over the black plastic.

"Don't you know—of course you don't. There's a thing known as caller id," she explained, pressing the button to end the call and the annoying signal. "That means, if the person you called has it, they will see my number displayed on their phone together with my name."

She waited, plainly expecting him to understand. It took a moment for revelation to strike. "Oh, shit," he muttered.

If, as he had worried earlier, the number belonged to the person who had tried to kill him or someone otherwise connected to that aspect of his life, they now had Meg's name and phone number. "But would that necessarily be something to worry about?" he asked, following his train of thought. "Would someone call back based on your number appearing on their phone? I don't quite get it. It's not like anyone would know I placed the call, would they?"

Drawing out the chair beside his own, Meg sat down. She set the phone on the table. "Of course not. Likely, at this hour especially, they would think it was a wrong number. To be honest, with the busy signal, I'm not sure the caller ID would even come up on the phone. If they had call waiting, yes, but not everyone does. The person whose number you called probably doesn't, or there wouldn't be a busy signal. I don't have it myself," she added, holding out her hand, palm up.

Caleb lifted a brow at her, confused by her gesture.

"The number on that paper," she said. "May I see it? Perhaps it's not even in this area code and you would need to dial a one beforehand, although I think you would get a message about that. There are ways to block the number you're calling from, too. We may as well keep trying until we get somewhere, right?"

Encouraged, Caleb spread the piece of paper with the scrawled number over her palm. She laid it on the table, holding the torn edges of the paper down with her thumb and index finger. Slowly, her head lifted. Her gaze, amazingly green even when deprived of sleep, held his.

"What?" he asked, alerted by her stillness.

"This," she stated quietly, "is my phone number."

Chapter 10

Her phone number. What the hell?

Meg looked again at the numbers he had written down to be certain, then back at Caleb. She could tell by his expression he was as shocked as she was by this development.

"I don't understand," he said at last.

Didn't he? But no. No, he didn't. She knew he didn't.

Rising from the chair, Meg moved stiffly to set the phone back in its cradle. She stood with her back to Caleb, thinking. She didn't understand either. Why would he "remember" her phone number? Was it subliminal from something he had seen? Perhaps she'd left her phone bill lying around, although she didn't believe that was the case. She'd certainly had a momentary doubt to his truthfulness, but it had occurred to her rather quickly that if he was shamming memory loss and knew her phone number for some reason that eluded her, he assuredly wouldn't be sitting at her table trying to dial it. What would be the point? But if her phone number was, in fact, a memory returned to him, why had he possessed it in the first place?

The other possibility, that he once again had read her thoughts, seemed doubtful. Thinking of her own phone number wasn't a conscious process of hers, at any rate.

"When did you recall this number?" she asked, turning around.

Elbows on the table, Caleb shoved his hands through his thick, dark locks. He paused to look up at her, eyes shadowed by his lashes. "Late in the afternoon. Before you came back."

Hmm. Late that afternoon she had been in town at the library and the grocery store, and she'd given her number to several people to call her if they'd heard anything about a ship going down in the area. Later, at the sailor's cross, she had spoken with Dan Stauffer. Dan had told her to call him, had asked her if she still had his cell phone number. At one point after that conversation, she had hoped Dan no longer recalled her number, a number that had come into her mind. Could it be that Caleb had picked up on any of that? Based on what she had learned over the years regarding telepathy, physical distance between subjects didn't hamper its occurrence. Separation didn't mean a damned thing.

Stunned, Meg sat down. That had to be it. The sharing of thoughts between them, though highly unusual, appeared to be the only explanation that fit.

She took one of his hands, drawing it down to the tabletop and interlacing her fingers through his. She eyed the newspapers she'd left earlier, covering the uneven marring in the table's surface, the words etched into wood by the vicious point of Matt's knife. She wouldn't think about them now.

"All of this will be sorted out in due course," she said.

"Due course? How long is 'due course'?"

She could see his frustration but no anger. She shook her head. "Who knows? I wish I could tell you that, but there's no way of knowing. Look, Caleb, despite the fact I work from home, I do try to keep a schedule and I need to be up early, so let's go back to bed now, all right?"

He didn't move. Obviously, he had decided he would go nowhere without more of an answer than she had given.

"How would I know your phone number?" he asked. "Tell me that."

"You picked it up subconsciously. Maybe it was written somewhere, or you heard me say it for some reason, or…I don't know."

"Is it possible I knew it? I mean, really knew it?" He squeezed her hand, his expression earnest and anxious.

"I don't see how. That would be one heck of a coincidence because we aren't acquainted. Well," she corrected, blushing, lifting his hand to kiss it, "we are more than acquainted now, but we weren't before. For you to have my phone number and end up on the beach outside my house might imply you were actually headed here, but I can't imagine why that would be. And if you weren't coming to me, to my home, then it would be too strange that you would end up here and carry with you in your minimal memory a knowledge of my phone number. Besides, I think—" She stopped, not quite sure she should tell him what she thought, but he insisted.

Meg exhaled. "Remember when I told you I dreamed certain dreams that come true?" Across from her, he nodded, tightening his grip on her hand again. "That, and other things, like knowing what a person is thinking—I mean truly knowing what a person is thinking—are considered to be aspects of a certain psychic ability. I don't believe there's any irrefutable scientific proof of these occurrences, although there has been plenty of study, and too many people experience such things to totally discount them as truth. I think you possess some ability yourself," she finished, waiting for his reaction.

He frowned. "Me? By saying this, you are suggesting this is not the norm, these psychic abilities?"

"Correct."

"And how does this explain the present situation?"

"In your case," she said, "I think you are reading memories and thoughts of mine, and with your own recall impaired, you are interpreting them as yours."

Releasing her hand, he stood abruptly, shaking his dark head. He stalked across the floor and back again. In jeans and nothing else, his battered body looked beautiful.

"All of them? All of my thoughts?"

"No. Only a few. Like my phone number," she hedged, hoping he wouldn't delve deeper, wouldn't question those moments she had recognized as belonging to her.

"Someone did try to kill me," he stated quietly. His eyes glittered in the light burning above the stove.

"Oh yes, I'm certain of that," she said. "There's no question that memory is yours."

"Why? Why isn't there any question?"

Pushing back her own chair, Meg stood and moved to stand in front of him. She put her arms around his waist. After a moment, he levered an arm across her shoulders, pulling her close to his chest. She turned her cheek against the soft, dark hair fanning out across his firm flesh.

"As frightening as it might be, it's your memory, Caleb. No one tried to kill me and the proof of violence done to you is visible." She did not mention what she had sensed when touching him earlier. She had no wish to confound him further.

His opened his mouth against her hair. She had to listen hard to hear the words he spoke. "I remember this, as well. Holding you."

"Shh," she whispered. "I don't have answers. I'm sorry."

He nodded against her. She breathed in the scent of him, pressing her lips to his chest.

"Will you think less of me if I tell you I'm afraid?" he asked.

"Never," she said against his skin. "Never."

In all honesty, their discussion had made her afraid, too.

* * * *

Standing in the doorway, Caleb made no noise. After the strain following their conversation in the middle of the night, he had been restless, revisiting the strange discussion over and over again, unable to sleep. He had been able to tell by Meg's breathing she slept fitfully, but when she awakened, she remained silent and physically apart from him. Now, in the light of day, he only wanted to know she was okay, with them, with herself. Instead, he found himself held in absolute stillness, watching the process of her work.

Stifling a yawn against the back of her hand, Meg turned the bristles of her brush through the paints on the palette. With sure strokes, she created the line of a picket fence running diagonally along the lower left corner of the picture. Several more strokes and she had the petals of flowers in the extreme foreground, followed by a dab of yellow at the heart of each, and then another brush with two shades of green for the foliage. She made it look easy. Caleb smiled, his gaze taking in the illustration as a whole. He didn't know the story, but he understood the little brown-haired girl skipping along the dirt lane with a battered doll in tow was headed home.

"Who's that?" he asked before he could stop himself.

Meg jumped. She glanced at him over her shoulder, looking as tired as he felt. Still, she smiled in that warm, sexy way she had, even when sex wasn't on her mind. His stomach lurched. He wanted to step close to her, bend and breathe in her scent.

"Hi," she said.

The distance of the night had passed. Relieved, he stepped into the room. "Hi."

Standing at her shoulder, he studied the picture again. The little girl looked familiar. With a start, he remembered where he had seen her before. Despite small differences, in essence she was the same child he had seen in several of the books Meg had illustrated.

"You've used her face in other books. She's a beautiful child. Is it someone you know? I mean, did you paint her from imagination or from life?"

Even as he spoke, he frowned. Odd how the peculiar vagaries of his affliction permitted him to recognize that concept but not who he was. Contemplating his question, Meg chewed on her lower lip before answering. At her side, a breeze ruffled the curtains at the open window, fluttering the hem of her shirt. Beneath the soft fabric, her shoulders shifted, altering her stance.

"In this story," she said, "her name is Molly. Her real name, though, is Anne."

"Anne?" Speaking the name, a reverberation thrummed through him to settle in his consciousness with unexplained weight.

"Yes. A simple name, and beautiful, neither old nor young. A name I figured she could never outgrow. And she never did."

The weight grew heavier. "What do you mean?"

"She's mine," Meg whispered.

"Yours...and Matt's?" A niggling of confusion surfaced. He had seen no sign of a child in this house.

Meg shook her head. "No. Matt wanted children, but after what happened, I couldn't. I didn't," she amended.

"What do you mean? What happened?"

Setting down the palette and the brushes, Meg moved to the window and sat before it in an old wooden chair. Caleb followed. He stood with his hand on the top of her head, fitting his fingers to the shape of her skull beneath her soft, honey-gold hair, reveling in the warmth of her scalp. She closed her eyes, tipping her chin up, her face to the sun.

"Before I moved here, before I met Matt, I had Anne. I wasn't married. I didn't care. It happened, and I had the baby. I never would have not had the baby, but once Anne was born, I was...I wasn't the same. I was a mom," she said with a sad smile. "It makes a difference."

Caleb stayed silent. The weight became an ache, taking his breath away.

"She died...away from me. Beyond my care. The young man who fathered her one day decided he wanted to share custody. I hadn't looked for anything from him, but he decided to grow up, I guess, to take responsibility, financially and physically. While she was with him, his car was struck by another that had run a red light. They were both killed."

A fall of tears washed down her cheeks. Lifting her bodily from the chair, he sat in her stead, settling her onto his lap and pulling her head down against his chest. Beneath their combined weight, the wood of the chair creaked in protest. The breeze from the window ran across the hair on his arms and through the locks beneath his stroking hand.

"I'm sorry," he said. Her loss touched him so keenly, he wondered if he might have children of his own, children he couldn't remember, children who would be missing their father. He buried his jaw, the curve of his cheek, into her hair, breathing deeply of its recently washed fragrance.

"I'm sometimes certain that's why he left me," she said softly. "Not the sea, not the myriad of other small things I recognized and he recognized, but the dark grief I carried around with me and the fact that I wouldn't… wouldn't give him a child. I didn't mean to hold that back from him. I was too scared, too afraid of the possibility of that loss again. You can't keep a child protected all the time. I know that you can't, but I don't know what to do with that fear."

He felt her swallow beneath the light grasp of his fingers along her throat, holding her close. "When did he leave?"

"Three years ago," she said. "I came home to a house devoid of all but those few clothes of Matt's that had been waiting to be washed, the ones you've been wearing," she said with a small, bitter laugh. "All of his personal belongings were gone. The funds in our checking account, too. The cash I kept hidden away for a rainy day was all I had left. There was a hastily scrawled note on the kitchen table with an address to send anything else I might come across but without explanation."

"None? He never said it had to do with your not wanting children?"

"No, he never said that. Yet there were many reasons, I suppose, for the both of us. He had changed. He made me afraid sometimes. No," she said again. "The only indication I had of a reason, and it wasn't really a reason, were the words 'I had to leave you.' But why?"

I had to leave you.

A small chill crept from the middle of Caleb's spine to the nape of his neck. *I had to leave you.* Those words were eerily familiar, haunting, making him cringe.

Meg went on. "Even now, I remember Matt's voice repeating that phrase a long time later as clearly as if he were speaking in my head this minute. It was the last time I spoke to him. The last time. Why didn't I ask him then what he meant? Why didn't I make him put it into words? Why didn't I tell him I was sorry? For that, at least. Only for that."

Caleb held her tighter. He lowered his chin onto the top of her head, turning to stare out the window. A glint of sun drew his gaze toward the deep shadow beneath the stand of ravaged pines to a car parked in the shadows. He could make out the sheen of the windshield, the curve of headlights. Looking at it, a frown formed on his lips, a surge of unexplained displeasure coursing through him. He pivoted away. Shifting his head, he pressed his mouth to Meg's crown.

"It'll be all right," he said. "You're strong. You've been strong."

She nodded against him. "And you're good for me, Caleb Hunter, no matter who or what the heck you are."

She laughed, a warm, silent burst of amusement. The crisis had passed. She was back in the light again. He could not help but think of the painting of the sea, of the dark tides in violet-hued depiction. Covered now by a cloth, that painting had nothing to do with her lost child. Nothing. She exorcized those demons regularly with light and lovely portrayals of her daughter in the guise of fictional characters. The threatening sea on canvas was another matter entirely.

"Come on," he said, stroking the lingering dampness from her cheeks, "clean up in here and I'll make us some breakfast."

"You will?"

"Sure. Nothing wrong with my short-term memory. You showed me how, remember? I'll even do the dishes."

She laughed out loud and he smiled, his heart hurting in his chest. He needed this from her. Needed her laughter, her joy, her trust, her... forgiveness.

For what? He didn't understand.

Chapter 11

"For the love of God, I'm fine! Get a doctor in here to sign me out, will you?"

The nurse eyed him over the black frame of her glasses as she made a notation in his chart. "I think not. Just keep your pants on. The doctor will be back to see you as soon as he's available."

"Considering I'm not wearing any pants, that's a pretty useless suggestion," Dan Stauffer muttered, throwing himself back on the emergency room bed. Folding his arms across his chest, he glowered at the nurse but failed to intimidate her. Once she had completed her task, and not one second sooner, she exited around the hanging curtain.

Glancing about, he spotted the fellow in the next cubicle grinning at him through the plexiglass divider, his hand lifted in the thumbs-up sign. Scowling, Dan laid his head back and closed his eyes.

Truth was, he wasn't fine, not for the love of God or anyone else. But he wasn't about to let anyone know it. All the tests had been negative, proving nothing was physically wrong. He had known that. When he'd managed to call for an ambulance, though, he'd been pretty sure he was about to die. Per his request, the ambulance had arrived without sirens or lights, and for a good two hours afterward, he still thought he might drop dead. When he finally realized he wouldn't, he knew he had to keep his mouth shut. He could never explain what had happened out there by Meg's place to anyone, least of all a medical professional who might develop the notion of committing him for a mental health evaluation. He'd be done. Career, reputation, all of it.

Memory of that shadow made him shiver. If it hadn't been so dark down by the sand he might have gotten a better sense of what he was looking at. Not that it mattered. The cold had gotten him, and the dread, and the impression of his very essence shrinking down to nothing.

No doctor in this hospital could assist him. He could imagine the result once skepticism gave way to a certainty he'd suffered a breakdown. He couldn't have that blot on his record. And he hadn't suffered any breakdown, or hallucinated, or fabricated in a moment of stress the whole incident. It had happened. He knew it had happened, and for the first time in his life, he gave real credence to the tales one occasionally heard of some poor soul being literally scared to death.

Had he been generally less healthy, he would be dead now. His heart would have exploded or fatally failed him in some fashion as adrenaline erupted into his system. The muscle wall surrounding the organ still ached, but the EKG had shown no change, no indication of heart attack.

Letting his breath out, Dan peered through slitted lids at the bed next door. Someone had pulled the curtain across and he could see the silhouette of a doctor moving around behind it. Not his doctor, though. Too tall. He closed his eyes again.

He didn't believe in ghosts. Never had. Never would, if asked. But he believed in something else now. He believed in the unexplained. Things happened, things that defied common sense, defied science, defied religion.

Ah, yes, religion. Tonight, he had prayed for the first time since he could remember. Prayed hard. Babbled bits and pieces of structured appeals, then made up his own as he went along, wanting only to be saved from that...that...that *darkness.* Shaped like a man, yet not a man at all but something... *Unholy.*

His heart, still hooked up to a monitor, began to race again. Dan breathed deeply, steadying his nerves. Wouldn't do to have his departure delayed. Not now. He had work to do and plenty of it.

Too bad they wouldn't allow him to use his cell phone here. He had calls to make first thing when he walked out the door. He needed to arrange for a couple of days off. Certainly, the doctor would be kind enough to write a note for him to take the time instead of admitting him into the hospital. It would be a bargain well struck. He would promise to be a good boy, go home and rest, if the doctor insisted he take a couple of days. Then he had to call the lab and get that chunk of wood that was in the back of his car tested. He had to call his ex-wife because she would learn he'd been in the hospital and would never let him hear the end of it if she didn't get the news first from his own mouth.

And then he had to call Meg Donovan and hope she would listen to him.

Chapter 12

For the third time that morning, Meg ignored the ringing telephone. If someone had information for her, he or she could leave a message. But the light on her answering machine remained red. This time, however, her cell phone chirped right after. Frowning, she let it go. After a moment, the soft twittering ceased, followed shortly by the signal that indicated she'd received a voice mail. Though inclined to ignore the message, she listened to it instead, shifting from the stool before her easel to stand by the window. She heard the creaking of floorboards in the living room as Caleb rose from the chair where he had been reading a children's book.

"Meg, it's Dan Stauffer. I need you to call me. I tried your landline and got no answer. Maybe you're out. However, it's important. I... It's important." His voice sounded strange, as if he wanted to say something more, but he finished up with a quick, "Call me when you get this message."

She had his number now and couldn't use that as an excuse not to call him back. Still, if he couldn't bother to be any clearer about the urgency of his message, she wouldn't bother to call him. Very likely, she hadn't been firm enough the other day when she'd run into him in town. It couldn't be official business, or he would have been at her door. Besides, there was no longer any reason for that. Matt was dead. The investigation had ended. Hadn't it?

"Everything all right?"

Caleb stood in the doorway, his head nearly brushing the frame, his dark hair tousled where he had been running his fingers through it. She hadn't trimmed it for him yet, but she rather liked it overgrown and unruly. The dark, silky ends curled along his neck. Odd how comfortable she'd become with his presence in her house, how familiar he already seemed. Meeting him under normal circumstances, she certainly would have been attracted to him, but if she had actually agreed to date him, it might have been months before she ever let him into her life like this.

"Fine," she said.

"Are you sure? You look concerned."

Concerned. How astute. She smiled at him, attempting to put him at his ease. She was concerned, but she didn't know why.

"Someone left me a message I wasn't expecting. One of the off—well, someone I know," she finished, not wanting to get into the details about the investigation into Matt's activities. Alleged activities, she reminded herself. Nothing had ever been proven, nor had she had the opportunity to clear the air with Matt before he'd left her. But she couldn't help remembering how the rumors had persisted, becoming ever more alarming once he moved to the town ten miles up the coast. Frightening, the chances people said he was taking. More horrifying to her were the whispers of more sinister activities, as if he didn't care about his life or anyone else's. She had tried to dismiss the stories outright, except... except the changes in him at the end made that impossible.

A shiver shook her from her reverie. "I think he wants to ask me out to dinner or something."

Caleb's head cocked to the side. "A...a date?" he asked, needing a few seconds to search for the right word.

"Yes," Meg said. "A date."

"Will you go?"

He didn't appear to be prying, only asking. Here again, the boundaries of their relationship blurred. Their association, though absolutely real in the physical sense, possessed less definition emotionally despite the underlying connection. Her lips twisted, and she took a step nearer to him, depositing the phone on the table as she passed. Stopping in front of him, she lifted her head to look into his eyes. "No. Even if I'd ever had an interest in doing so, I wouldn't. Not now."

A small smile played about his lips. He lifted a hand to toy with the strands of hair loosened from her ponytail, the heel of his palm against her collarbone. "Why is that?" he asked.

Her eyes narrowed. He knew her reasons. She could tell by his tone. For all that he couldn't remember, he obviously understood many things without explanation. His eyes had grown heavy, contemplative in a sexual manner. His respiration had become deep and slow. Her gaze roved to his mouth, the stubble of his jaw, then trailed down over his chest and along his jeans. She smiled. Though they fit him extremely well elsewhere, she noticed they were a couple of inches too short.

"What?" he asked, tipping his head to follow the direction of her gaze.

"Nothing," she said. He leaned closer. His breath feathered across her skin. She wanted to take his face into her hands and kiss him, long and deeply. Glancing down at his jeans again, she noted in the straining denim that similar thoughts ran through his mind. A slight tremor passed along the backs of her knees.

"I think we need to take a ride into town," she said.

"We do?"

"We do," she echoed. "If we're going to continue to do this," she said, stroking the evidence of his erection and feeling a rush of warmth at the rumbling sound of her name from deep in his lungs, "we need to go to the drugstore."

* * * *

Meg sensed his eyes on her, and when she glanced back toward the car she saw him watching through the smudged windshield. He had told her he liked the way she walked, sexy and carefree. His words pleased her more than she had admitted to him. At the doorway, she gave her hips a playful little shake and laughed in his direction, then yanked open the door and stepped inside. Shoeless, Caleb remained in the car wearing a pair of socks to keep his feet warm, having insisted on accompanying her into town, even when she had suggested he wait at home. She planned a stop at the discount store outside of town, where she would buy him a pair of shoes and some other items before they headed back. He had expressed dismay at her offer but, quite frankly, he was in need of more than the few clothes of Matt's he had been wearing.

Matt's clothes, Matt's bed, Matt's house. Meg shook off the frisson of chill dancing along her spine and strode to the back of the drugstore. They weren't Matt's clothes anymore, nor was it his bed, and the house belonged to her. For the first time in a long while, she made decisions that took into account an ownership of her own life. Doing so pleased her. Period.

Having reached the back of the store, she paused at the rack of condoms. Except that he was barefoot and probably wouldn't have had a clue how to go about it, she should have sent Caleb in to make this purchase. For one thing, embarrassment made her cheeks burn like a schoolgirl's, and for another, once she popped one of these boxes up on the counter, the entirety of the small town would likely know what she'd bought within twenty-four hours.

Turning her head, she eyed the woman behind the counter. Not someone she recognized. Good. Ridiculous, being embarrassed, but she couldn't help it. Responsibility was the smart thing, the right thing, but she hadn't had any need of birth control or protection since…well, since Matt. She'd been on the pill, then, and condoms were not in their repertoire. She didn't even know what type were the best to use.

"Crap," she muttered to herself.

Picking a box due to the attractive packaging, she gathered a few more items—deodorant, a new toothbrush, a comb—and set everything as unobtrusively as possible on the counter. As the cashier rang up her purchases, Meg dug in her purse for her wallet, aware with a flip of her stomach that someone had come up the aisle behind her. Trying for nonchalance, she snuck a sidelong glance from beneath her lashes as the customer came to a stop directly to her right.

"Meg."

Pausing in her hunt for cash, Meg glanced over her shoulder, drawing her breath in. Dan Stauffer's gaze moved from her eyes to the counter, where nothing had yet been bagged, and back to her face.

"The guy in the car can't buy his own?" he commented.

Meg didn't trouble to answer. Pulling out several bills, she paid the cashier, watching as the woman deposited everything into a plastic sack. Aware of Dan's continued and silent presence beside her, she turned to walk away with a nod to him and the cashier.

He stepped in front of her. "I called and left you a message."

Meg lifted her head. He had pushed his sunglasses up away from his eyes. Something about them, about his eyes, perhaps the dark circles beneath, the odd, shining intensity, made her pause instead of striding around him.

"I know," she said.

"Is there a reason you didn't call me back?"

"You didn't say what you wanted."

"I said it was important," Dan stated, harshness to his tone despite the flat delivery.

"You did," she admitted. "So what's up?"

He sucked in a breath, cut short. His gaze skimmed to the counter and the cashier. Meg glanced back to find the woman observing their exchange unabashedly. Without another word, Dan took her arm, steering her toward the front of the store and out onto the sidewalk. In her car parked out front, Caleb sat up. Giving a look she hoped he understood, Meg warned him to stay put.

"Let go of my arm, Dan," she said.

For a moment, she didn't think he would. His labored breathing sounded harsh in her ear, but he did finally release his grip above her elbow and dropped his hand to his side. With a dip of his head, his sunglasses dropped back into place. He turned as if staring at the street, but she could see his eyes in profile as they studied Caleb in the passenger seat of her car. A muscle in his jaw twitched. "Something happened the other night you need to know about."

Meg moved around in front of him, trying to call his attention away from her car and Caleb. "What do you mean?"

For several seconds, he didn't reply. His lips compressed, brows lowered as he continued to stare at Caleb. Under different circumstances, she might have asked him for help in searching for Caleb's identity. But not now. Not ever. She couldn't trust him.

After a moment, he turned to face her. "It's difficult to explain, but you need to know about it. Can I meet you later? Alone?"

He uttered the last word pointedly as Caleb opened the car door several inches. Dan kept his gaze on her now, despite Caleb's movements, as though dismissing him.

Meg shook her head. "No, there's no need. I can't imagine what you might have to say to me or why it would have to be alone. I don't think I want to know."

Clutching the drugstore bag and her purse, she pivoted on her heel and headed for the car. Once there, she yanked open the door and slid in behind the wheel. She fumbled the keys into the ignition and turned the motor over. Dan strode quickly to the driver's side door, bending toward the vehicle as she put the car into reverse. With her foot on the brake, she opened the window. Beside her, Caleb observed the scene with a contained expression, his posture alert, cautious.

Dan's blue eyes met Caleb's gaze. He nodded briefly. "I need to talk to your girlfriend. Do you mind giving us a moment?"

Meg spoke before Caleb had the chance to reply. "Dan, don't push it. I don't need to speak with you if I don't want to, do I? This isn't official, I take it. Your behavior is a bit inappropriate for an officer of the law."

"Damn it, Meg—"

"Dan, get away from my car. I'm leaving. Now."

His fingers curved over the edge of the window as he pressed his face into the small, open space. His expression made Meg's eyes widen.

"I found something out at your place—"

"What were you doing there?" she demanded, but he didn't pause.

"—that shouldn't have been there. From Matt's boat. The tides never would have brought it there. Never. And after—"

At his words, Caleb shifted, not toward Dan, nor away, but a small movement where he sat. Meg turned toward him. The sky darkened, the sun moving behind the clouds, dimming the interior of the vehicle. Meg thought of the painting of the dark tides and her addition to it, of the broken board bearing the name of Matt's fishing boat on it. *Jesus, oh sweet Jesus.* She closed her eyes. Whatever else Dan said became a buzzing din in her ears. A noise came from somewhere else, stifling sound and thought. Darkness filled her head, like night to her mind's eye, and she couldn't breathe.

* * * *

"Meg. Meg. It's all right. He's gone."

Opening her eyes, Meg looked at Caleb's fingers resting on her wrist. Dazed and nauseous, she turned toward the street, narrowing her eyes against the sun's glare. Dan was nowhere in sight.

"Where did he go?"

"He walked away. I guess he figured you weren't going to listen to him anyway."

Had it been that easy? She'd ignored him, and he'd given up? Yet, recalling the darkness, a tremor shook her from head to toe. Had she lost consciousness for some reason? It seemed she had because for a moment she'd been…well, gone.

But no, her foot remained steady on the brake, the car in reverse, her one hand on the steering wheel. If she'd blacked out, she would have gone limp, the car would have rolled back into the street, and Dan wouldn't have walked away.

"Are you all right to drive?"

Meg bit her lip. "I'll have to be. I assume you've driven at some point in your life, but I don't want to find out if I'm wrong by putting you behind the wheel."

Caleb made a noise in his throat, more amusement than concern. Ignoring him, Meg eased the car from the parking space and headed out of town, determined to finish the day's shopping. She didn't want to think about what Dan had been trying to say to her. Even so, as soon as she walked in the door, she sent Caleb upstairs with his packages and went to uncover the painting of the sea.

The bile rose in Meg's throat as her gaze fixed on the lower corner with the board bearing the name of Matt's boat visible beneath a sweep of water. What did this mean? Were they mistaken about where the ship had gone down? In the midst of a storm, Matt might have gotten confused, radioed the wrong coordinates, although all sorts of technology existed to prevent that happening. Still, was her painting an indication of some unexplained knowledge of that occurrence? No wonder she had temporarily lost her grip on reality when Dan had spoken. This perception of things beyond normal reckoning was horribly unnerving.

Precisely what had Dan Stauffer been doing on the beach near her house? Did he think because he was an officer of the law he had the right to trespass? And why had he been there? Oddly enough, her outrage served to steady her. She reached to pull the covering back over the painting. Behind her, Caleb's new shoes squeaked on the floorboards.

"I don't like that painting," he said. "It comes from somewhere absent light and hope. I don't like it at all."

Meg held out her hand. Caleb took her fingers between his palms.

"The painting has a name," she said. "I don't usually give titles to my works, but this one has a name. It's called 'Dark Tides.'"

"Dark Tides," he repeated without emphasis.

"Yes."

She stared at the painting a moment longer before flicking the sheet into place. She couldn't recall exactly when she'd begun the painting, although it hadn't been that long ago. When she'd started, she had worked at fever pitch into the small hours of the morning, as if driven. Now, she didn't even want to look at it. The painting made her think of things she'd rather not.

Like drowning.

Closing her eyes, she took a small step backward into the circle of Caleb's arms. She felt his thudding heart beneath her head and a slight tremor in his limbs. He saw what she had—she knew he did—the deep, dark liquid singing with silence. The draw of air that wasn't air, the panic, the release of hope, the moment of death.

With a sob, Meg broke Caleb's embrace. She spun around to face him, recognizing an unmistakable look of anguish, followed by nothing, his expression a blank stare above her head, eyes lightless.

"Caleb!"

She threw herself against him, frightened, beating his chest with her hands. He looked like the life had gone from him, except he stood right here in front of her. Not breathing. He wasn't breathing! She hit him again with the side of her clenched fist. The force staggered him backward and he opened his mouth, gasping a great lungful of air as he clutched the doorjamb for support. Coughing, he dropped to his knees. Meg crouched down beside him.

"Caleb look at me. Look at me!" she cried, and he raised his dark head. Meg swiped the dampness on her cheeks away with the back of her hand. "What did you see? Tell me. Tell me what you saw just now."

"I remembered...dying."

"What?" she said in shock.

"Dying in the ocean..." He shuddered. Meg wrapped her arms around him, drawing him against her shoulder.

"You didn't die in the ocean, Caleb. You're alive. You're here. If you weren't, it would mean I was sleeping with a ghost, and believe me, that's not the case. Oh, Caleb. I think I did that to you. I think I made you see that. My fear of what happened to Matt, the way I visualize it, must have..." God, why couldn't this affliction of hers be controlled? Could he have died from the vision she had unwittingly forced on him? No, that couldn't be possible. Because if it could... God, if that happened—

Sheering away from that consideration, Meg struggled to her feet with Caleb. When he swayed against her, she tightened her arms around him. "Let's get you upstairs," she said against his shirt. "You should lie down for a bit, okay?"

He didn't argue, which worried her more. Together, they climbed the stairs to her room, and she drew down the quilt. Caleb lay his long body on the bed. Meg tucked the blanket around his shoulders and smoothed the tangled hair back from his forehead.

"I'm sorry," she whispered.

Frowning, he shook his head, brushing off her apology.

"Should I call the doctor yet?"

"No."

Meg nodded without argument. "I'll sit here with you for a few minutes."

He stretched out his hand, pulling her down onto the bed beside him. Releasing a breath through her nose, she stretched out on top of the quilt, slipping an arm around his waist. She settled her head on his chest, listening carefully to the steady beat of his heart.

"Only for a few minutes," he agreed, pressing his lips to the top of her head. His fingers, calloused and strong, stroked tendrils of hair back from her face, her neck, before settling along the curve of her collarbone. Meg swallowed hard, fighting back tears. The cadence of his breathing beneath her arm gradually reassured her.

"Meg?"

"Hmm?"

"What are those things in that box? I knew everything else I was unpacking, but what the heck are they?"

Meg lifted her head a little to follow his gaze. On the night table against the lamp base stood the box of condoms. She sank her teeth into her lip to prevent a laugh, afraid there might be a touch of hysteria to it. Instead, she dipped her chin to plant a kiss on his firm, cotton-covered chest.

"I'll show you later," she whispered. "I promise."

Chapter 13

Meg leaned her forehead into her hand, tangling her fingers through her hair. In the darkened room, the computer screen shone like a ghostly beacon. She stared at it until her eyes hurt. Behind her, Caleb's breathing remained deep and even, his skin pale in the monitor's illumination. In an attempt to relieve her tired eyes, Meg glanced toward the parted curtain. Fat snowflakes struck the storm window like drifting shreds of gauze, while the shutters rattled against the clapboard. The Atlantic, driven wild by the winds of an early November storm, vibrated the earth beneath the foundations of the house. None of this appeared to be disturbing Caleb, who slept the slumber of the sated. She smiled at him tenderly.

Returning her attention to the article on the screen, she re-read the words she'd gone over countless times, not only in this article, but in others. Bluntly stated, sometimes an amnesiac's memory never returned to them. A little over two weeks had passed since Caleb had washed up on the beach, but he seemed no closer to recalling the lost details of his past life. They had settled into a routine, the two of them, comfortable and pleasant, and they rarely mentioned the fact that somewhere out there he'd left a life behind.

Apparently, no one from that life was looking for him, either. There had been nothing in the local papers, nothing on the news or on the web. No one sinister knocking at the door. Even so, the vision of him fighting for his life remained strong enough that when he had refused any advertisement of his whereabouts in the hopes of a response, she understood his reasoning. Not yet. Not until he remembered and knew what he was dealing with.

If he remembered, she mused, staring again at the monitor.

Caleb made a noise in his sleep, rolling his head. Shutting down the computer, Meg went back to bed. Shirking out of her slippers and robe, she climbed beneath the covers and snuggled against his side, sliding her fingers into the curly, silky hair on his chest. Outside the wind continued to blow, snow whispering along glass. Inside, hot water ticked through the pipes, heating the old radiators. Caleb breathed in and out beneath her hand in a slow, steady rhythm.

She kissed the flesh beside his chill-puckered nipple with a flick of her tongue, thinking how much she needed this, needed this closeness. The strange and abrupt circumstance of their relationship had ceased to trouble her. There would be much to consider in the future if they continued together, but for now, she was content to let those concerns wait until necessity dictated otherwise. Bound in a warm interlude that would, in time, change to become something else, for now they had fulfillment and peace.

Unexpectedly, she thought of Dan Stauffer. Whatever he had wanted, he had not troubled her further. As far as the fragment of wreckage he had located, if he had anything more to tell her on that subject, she had no doubt he would. But he hadn't. He hadn't called her or showed up at the house. She wondered if it had been some sort of ruse to get closer to her.

Biting her lip, she ignored the unrest caused by her recollection of the abrupt end to the conversation at her car. For some reason, that fragment of time remained unclear to her. As for what had taken place afterward with Caleb, when he remembered drowning, well, she had been careful ever since to keep a rein on certain thoughts. So far, that tactic appeared to be working remarkably well.

Snuggling closer into the heat of Caleb's armpit on her naked shoulder, Meg blew a concentrated breath across his chest, watching goose bumps stipple his flesh. With the tip of her tongue she tested the texture of his skin and lightly stroked his nipple.

"Meg," he mumbled sleepily, "what are you doing?"

"Nothing," she whispered. "Go back to sleep."

He did so, a testament to his exhaustion. Grinning, she pressed closer to him, listening to his breathing. Fitting her fingers against the arch of his rib cage, she then moved them gently along the lowest rib, careful not to tickle him, and into the ridge of soft hair that ran up from his groin. In the blackness beneath the covers, she slid her hand downward to the place from which the majority of his heat emanated. Flaccid flesh curved into her palm, and she held him for a moment, keeping her hand still.

Where had this man come from, this man who banished the loneliness from her life, with whom she kept good company, who gave her pleasure? A stranger and yet not a stranger, and even the idea of his strangeness thrilled her as she cupped his heavy, sleeping penis in her hand. If he woke up now, would he be offended by her familiar handling of him while he remained unaware? She didn't think so.

Smiling still, she unfurled his penis against his abdomen and began to stroke him leisurely with her curled fingers. A slight alteration in his breathing indicated his awareness, though he slept on as blood began to engorge his flesh. Knowing that what she planned to do next would likely drag him out of his much-needed slumber created a twinge of pleasurable guilt as she slid down beneath the covers.

As she ran her tongue along the length of a growing erection, his hand shot down beneath the covers and into her hair. She shivered as a moan rumbled through him, but he didn't make her stop. Of course not. Why would he?

Smiling against his firm flesh, she continued in her pursuit, every sound that escaped him evoking a responding vibration from her throat. The heat of his entire body increased with his stimulation. The hair of his thighs beneath her palms lifted at her touch.

"Meg."

She laughed against him.

"*Meg.*"

Resting her chin against his hip, she flipped off the covers. "Yes?"

"I have a question."

Her brows arched. "Now?"

"Uh-huh."

"Oooo-kay."

Scrambling onto her knees, Meg straddled his thighs, draping the quilt over them both, holding it against his chest with one hand and continuing to caress him with the other.

"Go ahead," she said. "Ask."

"Can you stop that a minute?"

Feeling chastised, she did. "Sorry."

"Don't be sorry," he whispered. "I love what you do to me. But I…I can't think when you're doing that."

She smiled in the darkness. Against the windowpanes, the snow continued to whisper and the shutters rattled, increasing her sense of isolation from the rest of the world here, with him, in her house by the sea.

"Don't you want something more from me?" he asked.

"What do you mean? You don't think I only want you for this, do you?" she asked, tightening her fingers around him again. He made a small sound, like a growl, deep in his chest.

"I should be helping you around here. I feel damned useless. Give me something to do."

"I am giving you something to do," she murmured, pressing herself against him. Before he could be insulted by her statement, she added, "There's plenty that needs doing, but the weather isn't right for it. In the springtime, all the trim will need painting, the gardens reworked, then..." She sighed, looking at him in the silvery gloom. His eyes, shadowed by his lashes, appeared black.

"Will I be here in the springtime?"

"I don't know. I'd like you to be."

"Me, too," he stated quietly.

Bending forward, she planted her hands on his chest and kissed him. "I don't have any idea where we're going," she whispered against his mouth. "There are too many unknowns, too many variables. You could have someone waiting for you, you know?"

"I hope not," he said, his breath drifting around the hollow of her mouth. "I think I want only you."

At his words, tears pricked her lids. He drove both hands into her hair, pulling her mouth down hard against his. His tongue moved languidly, and she recalled all he had been doing with it since they'd met. Her thighs trembled, slick with the moisture of her arousal. Rolling, he positioned his body on top of hers, his thick cock between her legs, the tip pressed against her labia.

"How could we have not known each other?" he asked in an undertone. "It's like I've always been here, like your body and mine have always conformed to each other, belonged together, like this," he said, sliding into her.

"Oh," she whispered, his heat spreading rapidly into her veins. She reached for the box on the bedside table.

"No. Wait. Please, wait. I want to feel you this way for a moment. It's so much better like this."

"I know, but—"

"Wait a bit," he said again and began to move with torturous precision, in so far, then out, nearly free of her, hovering as if in indecision, before gliding back home. Over and over while she lay nearly still, held down by his body, by the weight of sensation, of fire flooding her abdomen, her limbs, as he slowly slipped in and out, in and out, with a timing that made her tremble.

"Caleb—"

"Shh."

If he had changed his pacing, shifted his weight, she might have been able to come back from the place where she had drifted, but he was deliberate in his actions. In and out, unbearably hot and slow, inexorably timed like the foaming surf of the ocean, relentless and endless and consuming.

"Caleb—"

"Go ahead, sweetheart," he whispered.

"Caleb—"

"Shh."

Bound by the motion of his entry and retreat, she gazed at him in the darkness, at the sweat-sheen of his skin, his hair grown damp. His pupils dilated with his effort at control. A single drop of perspiration fell from his brow onto her erect nipple, running over the curve of her breast.

"Oh, God," she moaned, arching against him.

When she came, she dragged him to her, wrapping her arms around his neck with her mouth open on his as she cried out again and again, hearing his voice echo her release as he drove her down to a place where the silver light of the falling snow shattered and vanished.

* * * *

When Meg awoke in the morning, she knew she had been dreaming of Matt. She had watched him lie beside her in their bed, telling her about the child he had wanted. Odd, the way dreams worked. Sometimes it was as if you were standing on the sidelines as on observer, not a participant. Closing her eyes, Meg touched her stomach, low, then slitted her lids to cast a glance at the box of condoms, retrieved from the place where it had fallen the night before. She thought of the possibility of pregnancy and closed her eyes again.

"Please," she whispered, not entirely certain what she was asking for.

What a betrayal of memory that would be, to deny her husband the child he had wanted, only to conceive in a coupling of uncontrolled lust with a man she barely knew.

Amazed at the bitterness of her reflections—especially after her closeness to Caleb the night before—Meg tossed back the covers and got out of bed. The other side of the tousled bed lay empty. The door to the hallway stood open.

"Caleb?"

She went to the door and put her head out.

"Caleb?"

Hearing noise in the kitchen, she called down the stairs as she headed into the shower, "Good morning!"

His muffled reply sounded with friendly reassurance. She didn't want her strange mood to be catching. Standing in the bathroom, waiting for the water to heat up, Meg looked out the window at the frigid coating of November snow sparkling on the roof shingles and scattered across the sparse, sandy lawn. Most of the precipitation appeared to have blown into sheltered areas and gathered there, leaving the road clear. Maybe she would give Caleb another driving lesson today. Re-lessons, surely, considering how fast he seemed to be picking it up.

Stepping into the shower as the steam started to roll across the ceiling, she took her time bathing, washing her hair, wondering if last night might have been enough to get her pregnant. It only took once, after all. One time, one narrow-tailed, swimming little sperm. In the future, she would have to be more careful. Even if she considered herself ready, which she didn't, to put Caleb in the position of being a father would not be fair to him. He might already have an entire brood, for all they knew. And if he didn't, it didn't matter. Until he had some idea who he was, how could he be certain what he wanted in his life?

Turning off the shower spray with wrinkled fingers, Meg toweled dry and wrapped her hair, then moved to the mirrored cabinet for her comb. Written with a finger on the steamed glass, she found a heart with an arrow thrust through it, together with a set of initials, interlinked. Though dripping, they remained clear enough to read. *M.D. and M.D.*

Neither one of them belonged to Caleb. In years gone by, she had seen this heart, these matching initials side by side, written in the steam by her husband while he shaved and she showered. Her heated skin stippled with chill.

"No," she whispered, suddenly lightheaded. Her legs gave out and she dropped onto the closed lid of the toilet, pressing her head between her knees. "No," she breathed again.

What the fuck was going on? Battling an overwhelming desire to vomit, Meg raised her head to stare at the melting heart on the mirror. Had she made it happen again? Was she thinking so hard about Matt, the possibility of a baby, and Caleb's position in her life that she had caused him to do this? She hadn't heard him come in, but he could have entered quietly while the water was running. Could have? Caleb must have come in. It could only have been his finger marking the glass in a long-forgotten ritual from her newlywed days. After all, she hadn't done it. And it sure as hell hadn't been Matt.

Hearing footsteps in the hall, Meg jumped up and wiped the edge of her towel across the mirror. Confronting Caleb with evidence of something he likely wouldn't remember or understand doing would be of no help to him. She opened the door when he knocked. Drifting at ceiling height, steam rolled out past his head into the hallway.

"I made us breakfast," he announced with a grin. A white substance resembling powdered sugar spattered his shirt and clung to the hairs on his right arm.

"Again? You're quite the homemaker," Meg said in an attempt to cover her lingering disquiet. "Thank you."

Leaning into the bathroom, he kissed her forehead. "You're welcome."

Wrapping her arm around his neck, she breathed in his scent, pressing her lips to the side of his throat.

"Caleb…"

"Yes?"

"Nothing," she said. "Never mind. Let me get dressed and we'll eat."

"All right," he answered, stepping away. "And then would you mind giving me a quick refresher on the computer? I always balk at the same point after I get the damned thing turned on. I'm good after that, though."

"Sure," she agreed, forcing a smile. With any luck, he might find something she'd missed. The sooner he found out anything about his life, the better off they both would be.

Chapter 14

Hunt-and-peck, Meg called the way he typed words on the keyboard. Even so, he was growing more adept at the task every day. Somewhere, he had done this before. Even searching the Internet seemed vaguely familiar. The spelling of words came back to him the more he worked. Having grown tired of dead ends regarding his own name, finding people who didn't resemble him in the slightest or who had been dead for many years, he had typed in Meg's name and discovered an abundance of information about her. Articles about her work, places where books she'd illustrated were sold, interviews. She even had her own…what was it called? Website. The authors of the books she'd illustrated had their own websites as well, chatty and personal, whereas Meg's was all about her work and very little about herself.

Her picture was on it, though. She was standing on the back porch of this house, looking pretty and extremely feminine in a loose, pale dress. A breeze had blown her bangs into her eyes, and she was laughing. He loved her laugh. Sometimes, he felt like he loved her. Could that be possible?

Sitting with his elbows on his knees and his hands interlaced beneath his chin, he stared at the picture with the caption, "Megan Donovan, Illustrator of Children's Books."

"Oh, you found that, did you?"

He glanced sheepishly over his shoulder as Meg deposited the laundry basket in the middle of the bed. He pointed at the monitor. "You look happy in this picture."

"I was." She sounded perplexed by the admission. A twinge of something, almost anger, pricked him at her tone. He pushed it away.

"Do you want me to put those clothes away for you?"

"If you want. They're folded, so there's no hurry. I'm going to get to work."

"Okay," he said, listening to her footsteps as she retreated from the room. Once she had gone, he lifted a finger to touch the two-dimensional face on the monitor. She did look happy. What had happened?

Gazing at the screen, he decided there might be a way to find out. Going back to the search engine she had showed him, he typed in her husband's name.

"Shit," he muttered. Apparently, Matt and Donovan were commonly paired names. Maybe if he added something else to the parameters, like the name of Donovan's fishing boat. What was it? He could find out if he checked the painting of the sea, but she would catch him at it. Not only that, but he didn't find the idea of looking at the painting again particularly appealing. Had he noticed the name of the town at any point? Not that he could recall, and Meg's website made no specific mention of it.

Sitting back on the low stool in front of the coffee table, which served as a desk in the bedroom, Caleb let a breath out over his lips. He lowered his arms to his thighs, drumming his fingers on his knees.

"Shit," he said again. He stood up from his uncomfortable position on the stool and stretched the length of his body.

Frowning in thought, he walked to the bathroom. Flipping up the lid of the seat, he unzipped his pants, turning his head to glance out the window. Two cars traveled close together along the roadway at a low speed, slowing further as they approached Meg's house. In instinctive, unexplainable reaction, Caleb re-zipped his pants and took a sideways step away from the window, keeping an eye on the cars. "Hello," he breathed. "Who's this?"

The cars pulled into the driveway, out of his line of sight unless he exposed himself to view. He waited, counting the doors opening and closing. Three. Three people got out of those two cars. A short interval later, he heard the sound of knocking on the door below. If Meg was in the little room where she painted, it would take her a moment to reach the front of the house. Caleb headed toward the top of the front stairs, avoiding in his swift stride the places where the floorboards squeaked. Standing with his back to the wall, holding himself steady to make no betraying noise, he waited for Meg to open the door.

Her heavy socks whispered along the hardwood floor as she talked to herself in a quiet voice. At the door, she paused, no doubt looking out before opening it. *Good girl.* If she called his name, he would be down there in a heartbeat. If not, he would assume someone she knew had come. He was thrown, however, by her hesitation before opening the door. She seemed reluctant, swearing under her breath. Why?

He heard the sound of the latch and the slight squeaking of the hinges as she drew the door inward. She didn't open the door all the way. Caleb tensed.

"Dan?" she said. "What's going on?"

Dan. The guy from town. Anger surged through Caleb, unexpected and strong. The hallway dimmed around him. *Breathe*, he told himself. What was his problem?

"Meg Donovan," stated the man in a voice meant, for some reason, to sound official, but Caleb could hear something underlying his tone, some severe emotion he attempted to hold in check. Caleb would have thought it fear if he could fathom any reason for it. When Meg didn't answer, Dan repeated her name. Idiotically, it seemed to Caleb.

"Of course. You know me. What's going on?" she repeated.

Risking a quick check, Caleb peered around the wall and ducked back again. Three men stood in the doorway, not exactly patient in stance. The one, Dan, was not dressed as he had been in town, but wore a uniform of some sort. A police uniform. Yes, a police uniform. The other two wore suits.

One of the other men spoke. "Agent Phillips, Mrs. Donovan. May we come inside to speak with you, please?"

"Agent Phillips? With what agency are you affiliated?"

"FBI, Mrs. Donovan. Would you like some identification?"

"If you don't mind, yes, I would."

"Of course. And this is Agent Andre."

A shuffling of position and, it seemed, identification had been produced because Caleb heard Meg step back and the squeak of the door opening wider. "Come into the kitchen. Dan…I mean, Officer Stauffer, knows where it is. I'll put some coffee on."

Caleb listened to the footsteps moving to the back of the house and followed them to the top of the kitchen steps. Unfortunately, the door at the bottom had been shut. He could hear the four voices, three masculine and one soft and feminine, but not what they said. Frowning at the staircase, he realized there wasn't a single silent tread on the whole flight.

For a moment, he contemplated going down the front stairs in order to hear the conversation, then he remembered that the door below had been open when he went to the bathroom. Meg must have closed it upon entry into the kitchen. Either she didn't want him to hear what they were saying, or she wanted to make certain they didn't hear him. The latter seemed the more likely scenario. After a brief debate with himself, Caleb retreated to Meg's bedroom. Silently, he returned to the seat before the computer and began typing in a new set of inquiries.

* * * *

At least they were polite, Meg thought as she measured out the grounds into the coffeemaker. She was stalling and they probably knew it, but she couldn't begin to imagine what these men wanted from her, and she needed a few minutes to collect herself. She was frankly surprised they were giving her any time at all.

"Sit down," she said over her shoulder. "I'm almost finished here."

When she looked back, they still stood, even Dan, who appeared nervous as a hare. His eyes kept darting to the beach outside the window, his breathing uneven, the standard bulletproof vest beneath his light blue shirt creaking. Telltale dampness seeped out from his armpits. The thermometer affixed to the outside of the glass read thirty-six degrees. No reason to be sweating.

If anyone should be sweating, it should be her. Oddly enough, now that the initial shock of the three men appearing at her door had begun to wear off, an icy calm had taken over. She took her time removing four mugs from the cabinet and set them on the counter, followed by the sugar bowl and the half and half from the refrigerator. Behind her, the men shifted in silence where they stood, but still they didn't sit.

Water the color of cola ran down through the filter, slowly filling the Pyrex pot beneath. Meg removed spoons from the drawer, napkins from the closet. She pulled out a box of cookies and prepared to arrange them on a plate.

"That's not necessary, ma'am."

"No? None of you would like any? Dan?"

He shook his head. His eyes slid to the counter and then to her breasts. Meg cleared her throat and he looked away. The one who had introduced and identified himself as Agent Phillips lifted a briefcase and laid it down on the table. He raised the lid and removed several photographs. Closing the case, he set the photographs on top, face down.

Before Agent Phillips had flipped them over, none of the photographs appeared to Meg to be of the board bearing the name of Matt's boat. When they'd arrived, she'd figured these men had come about the wreckage being in the wrong spot, or whatever it was Dan had been babbling about the other day. She didn't think so now. Though she'd only caught a glimpse of the photos, they had people in them. Pressing her tongue against the back of her teeth, Meg returned to preparing the coffee, asking each man how he preferred his.

Meg handed each man his cup in turn, then moved to the table with hers and stood beside one of the empty chairs.

"Sit, Mrs. Donovan," said Agent Phillips.

"Certainly," she replied. "If you will."

The third man, the one called Andre, an Interpol agent, frowned at her words.

Holding her cup, Meg took a small sip, turning her lips up with deliberation into a polite and patient smile. Finally, Agent Phillips sat down, followed by the other agent, and then Dan. That battle won, Meg pulled out the chair at her side and sat, too.

She knew this game. She had played it before and not well. Let no one say she had not learned from her mistakes.

After several gulps of coffee, dutifully ingested, Agent Phillips lowered his cup with care to the table. Taking the photographs from the top of the case, he shuffled them in his hands before fanning them out in a close, overlapping arrangement between his coffee cup and Meg's. Meg leaned forward, eyebrows raised. She deliberately avoided looking at the pictures. The last thing she wanted to do was betray her emotions to these men.

"Yes?" she said, holding her gaze steady on Agent Phillips' face.

"Kindly take a look at these surveillance photographs, if you would, Mrs. Donovan. They've been taken over the past several months in the Bahamas and off the coast of the Carolinas. Identify anyone you might recognize."

Surveillance photographs? Her gaze snapped down, not quite focused. She blindly extended her hand and dragged the photos closer. She turned them face up.

Caleb. She had expected they would be of Caleb, all recent events considered. But they weren't.

"Oh, my God," she breathed as the air shimmered into unbearable brightness.

* * * *

They'd gone. At one point there had been a certain amount of commotion, what seemed like chairs sliding across the floor and raised voices, before all had been calm again. The muffled conversation droned on and on until he heard thudding footsteps exiting the kitchen, the front door open and close, the car engines start, the crunching of tires as the vehicles left the driveway. Caleb watched from the bathroom window, far enough back to be unobserved, as the two cars drove off down the lonely, winding stretch of road. He had waited for Meg to come up and tell him what had happened. Instead, a short time later, he'd heard the back door shut and Meg's racing steps across the porch. Now, he stood at her bedroom window and watched her out on the sand by the water's edge.

Bundled in a coat and scarf, she paced above the surf line, stopping every so often to stare out toward the gray horizon, her hands shoved deep into her pockets. Rocking on his heels, Caleb kept his gaze glued to her as he thought about what he had learned confined to the silence of her bedroom. FBI stood for Federal Bureau of Investigation. He had read their mission statement, knew their jurisdiction, and read about their headquarters and their satellite offices throughout the country. He knew who Dan Stauffer was, too, and his connection to Matt Donovan and to Meg. An article from a local newspaper told how Office Stauffer had come to the house, together with a representative of the Coast Guard, to tell Meg about her husband's ship going down with all hands. With all hands. Caleb wasn't sure what that meant until the point had been clarified later on. Matt and all the men on board with him had died. A tiny, poorly defined photograph accompanied the article, showing four men standing in front of a boat, their faces indistinct.

Meg dropped abruptly to her knees in the sand, her face in her hands. Caleb's chest tightened. He pulled on his shoes and grabbed his coat— the one she had bought for him, not Matt's sweatshirt jacket—and raced down the stairs, hurrying out to her. Running in sand was not the easiest thing to do. It was like slogging through a dream, his mind racing ahead to his destination while his legs kept dragging him backward. All the while, Meg sat slumped on the ground above the tide line unaware of his approach, unaware that he cared so much about her already his heart broke to see her weeping.

"Meg!" He stumbled toward her and scooped her up into his arms, holding her tight against his chest. She buried her face against the suede of his jacket, shoulders heaving in his embrace. He smoothed her hair back, his palm dampened by the salt tears streaming along her cheeks.

"Meg," he said again, softer now, his voice almost lost in the sound of the surf. "What's wrong? What happened?"

She continued to cry, fingers curled into the fabric by his jacket zipper and in the hair at the nape of his neck. He held and rocked her, watching the gulls circling overhead, the sun a pearlescent disc in the clouded wintry sky beyond.

Celia Ashley

"It's freezing out here," he said in time. He felt her nod against him, her hair soft beneath his hand. His breath plumed. "Do you want to go inside?"

"In a minute," she mumbled.

He pulled her closer, enveloping her to keep her shivering body warm. He turned his jaw against her head, against the hair at her crown, breathing in the scent of her shampoo rising from her heated scalp.

"What happened?" he asked again.

She drew a deep, shuddering breath in the circle of his arms and stepped back. He let her go. Lifting her head, she met his gaze, her green eyes wet, shining, and ravaged.

"He hated me."

Caleb didn't ask who she meant. He knew.

"I always thought there was a possibility he didn't, that things weren't good enough between us to keep us together, but I was wrong. He hated me."

"How do you know that?"

She inhaled again and released the breath in a long sigh that frosted the air in front of her mouth. "No matter what, he should have known I would be devastated when word came to me he died. And all this time, he let me believe."

Caleb experienced a chill under his coat that had little to do with the temperature. "Let you believe what?"

"That he was dead, Caleb. He's not. Matt's alive."

Chapter 15

Suddenly everything had become different, skewed, warped. Nothing made sense. Matt had never died, never gone down in his boat in the vast, cold ocean. All her obsessions about his drowning, her fears for him, her grief became pointless. Her daily rituals for the repose of his soul had been a futile exercise. The happiness that had begun in Caleb's arms was false because she had thought herself free of Matt, that Caleb had freed her, but he hadn't, she wasn't. Matt was still out there, living a life, an apparently criminal life, not caring that she thought him dead, not caring that the connection she thought broken between them at last had only been masked by a cruel deceit.

Caleb sat beside her on the sofa holding her fingers in his chilled hand, saying nothing, both of them positioned stiffly, bundled still in their coats. Desolation hung like a solid manifestation in the air between them, and she couldn't understand why.

After a few minutes, Caleb released her hand and put his arm around her shoulder, pulling her snug against his body. He unwound the scarf from her neck and began to unfasten the buttons of her coat. She caught the heavy zipper tag of his jacket between her thumb and forefinger and tugged it down. Cool air smelling of the sea rushed from the weave of his garment. Fighting back a sob, Meg stood up, forcing the sleeves down his arms, jerking out of her own coat. She stood before him breathing heavily. The eyes he raised to hers were heavy lidded and sad in the half-light of the room. Why? Why did any of this have to matter to them?

With head-spinning swiftness, Meg threw her arms around Caleb's neck and straddled him, knees sinking deep into the cushion to either side of his thighs. She pressed her lips to his face, his neck, his mouth in rapid succession, murmuring frantic words as the salt fluid of tears mingled with the liquid heat of their tongues. Fingers curled, she dragged at his shirt, heard the snap of thread along the seams, and pushed him harder against the back of the couch. His breath rushed into her lungs. A long, slow quiver ran the length of his body, and he encircled her upper arms with his large hands, setting her back onto his knees. Startled and uncomprehending, she opened her eyes to the anguish in his own, silver trails of tears on his skin.

The flash heat of lust and desperation vanished in a chill as cold as the tide-washed sand on the shoreline. "Caleb, I'm sorry," she whispered.

Caleb nodded, one side of his mouth curving in understanding. Meg reached out to wipe the moisture from his face before folding her hands in her lap.

"Do you love him?" he asked.

Meg stared at the beautiful, rugged face of the man without a past, the man who had washed up onto her beach like a gift and who she had accepted into her life. The bitter wind outside the window at his back seemed to grow still, as did the sounds all around them. Blood coursed through her veins in an audible rush.

This, of course, explained the shift in the world, defined why Matt's existence had to matter to them. If she still loved the husband who had abandoned her, the husband she had pushed away, who had run from her, from the two of them together, who she had held in her heart as dead for over a year, then it made a difference to what she and Caleb had now. It made all the difference.

Did she love Matt? Not an easy question to answer. She couldn't give Caleb unconditional assurances she did not, nor could she say yes. Did she want Matt back? She had, once upon a time, but she had stopped wanting that long ago. Yet, if Caleb hadn't been here and she'd received the news she had today, how would she have reacted? Did she recognize the love she had borne Matt Donovan for years, beaten and twisted by the darkness that had touched their lives? Yes. But did she love him still?

Sliding her fingers between Caleb's, she squeezed them. He squeezed tighter.

"Caleb—"

"Don't," he said. "Don't answer the question I asked you. It's not fair. There's no decision to be made here, no choice between me and a man you thought was dead and have found out is not. Besides, I'm temporary, right?"

No, she mouthed, not true, but nothing came out. *Not temporary*, she wanted to say. *What about the springtime? You wanted to be here come springtime, and I wanted you here, too.*

Keeping the words inside, she started to cry again, angry with herself for doing so. Caleb pulled her down against his chest, pinning her with one arm while the other continued to hold her hand.

"Should I leave, do you think?"

"No," she said. "Stay. Stay here with me."

"But it's not the same now, is it?"

"No," she whispered, the muscles around her heart contracting.

Matt's absence or Matt's presence made small difference to the manner in which he colored her life. She hated him for not being dead, for tipping the balance she had begun to find again.

Closing her eyes, she clung to Caleb's warm body while he held her, not wanting to get up from that couch, not wanting to face what might come next.

* * * *

"It's snowing again."

Unusual weather, this, so early in the season. Unlike the storm the night before, this one flew in earnest. She wouldn't be sleeping nude beside Caleb tonight in the freezing house.

Meg bit her lip. There would have been no sleeping nude beside Caleb tonight anyway.

Turning from the window, she studied Caleb's back. He looked like a lanky praying mantis seated on the low stool in front of the computer, his knees drawn up, his arms stretched between them to the keyboard. Searching the Internet had become his fixation, and how could she blame him? If she'd been in his place, the search for information would have been paramount. Right now, he read about Interpol, not surprising because she had informed him the third man came from that agency. She walked up to stand behind him. On impulse, she placed her hand on his shoulder. Without hesitation, he turned his head and kissed her thumb.

She smiled in a surge of…of what? Gratitude, maybe. Whatever it might be, her heart lifted. Dropping to her knees behind him, she put her arms around his waist, leaning her head against the ridges of his spine. "Find anything interesting?"

"It's all interesting to me," he answered, fitting the fingers of his left hand into hers while he continued to peck around the keyboard with the right. She smiled against him, breathing in the scent of deodorant and warm flesh. "You're not cold?"

"Nope." She could hear the answering smile in his voice.

"I am," she said.

"Get in bed. I'll be there soon."

Comfortable, familiar, as if nothing had changed. If they could work hard enough at keeping change at bay, maybe it wouldn't happen. A foolish hope. Everything changed. Life was not static. What those changes were and what you did with them were what mattered.

Rising, Meg undressed in haste and slipped into her favorite ratty sweats and a sweatshirt, then pulled a pair of socks on over her feet. She leaped off the cold floor into the bed, burrowing under the covers. When she poked her head back out, she found Caleb watching her. He smiled, but she saw no humor in his eyes.

Oh, Caleb, she called silently to him. She stretched her hand out. Mutely, he rose from the stool, stretching his cramped limbs. He came to the foot of the bed and crawled across the mattress to her, halting with his face above hers. His dark, tangled hair hung forward across his eyes, shadowing them, making them look darker than the hazel she knew. She couldn't read their expression.

"Too many unknowns, you said. Too many variables. I need to find out who I am, Meg. We'll know what to do then."

Meg swallowed. She touched her finger to the length of his shaven jawline and nodded. He kissed her, not so much with passion as with promise, before climbing beneath the covers and stretching his long body alongside hers. Folding her in his arms, he pulled her close.

"Shit. I forgot to turn off the computer."

"It's fine," she said. "It'll enter sleep mode on its own in a little while."

Grunting, he reached to the bedside table and switched off the light. The only illumination came from the blue–white glow of the monitor. Snowflakes flew with crystalline delicacy against the windowpanes. He pressed his lips to the side of her head, the breath from his nostrils sweeping single strands of hair in its wake.

"Meg, it'll be all right," he whispered.

"Okay," she said. "Okay."

He snuggled down into the pillow. His body relaxed. She glanced at him. The lashes of his closed lids lay thick and dark against his skin.

Okay, she said again to herself. It's okay. This is where we are.

Chapter 16

Snow lay inches deep on the beach. Spume from waves seeped into the ice, making it pocked and dirty looking before disappearing into the receding sea. Most years, the sand would retain the sun's warmth better than grass and would not let precipitation accumulate, but the days prior to the storm had been gray and unseasonably cold. Abandoning the surf, gulls bobbed on ocean swells warmer than the air above. Wrapped in a shawl, feet shoved into a pair of unlaced boots, Meg watched the scene from a vantage point against the porch railing. Webs of snow drifted across the cleanly swept boards. Beyond, the garden had been transformed by the weather into something unrecognizable but lovely.

Huddled beneath the draped garment against the cold, Meg found herself recalling a day shortly after she and Matt had married, young and still in love, thrilled by the romance of the first snowfall, of their first winter together. He had wanted to give her flowers, but he couldn't get his hands on any, so he fabricated them from white facial tissue out of the bathroom and set them on the cleared porch for her to find when she stepped outside. "Snow flowers" he had called them, laughing at his creation. She had saved every one, pressed flat in an old book for years.

Sighing, Meg brought the shawl close to her face, burying her eyes against the soft knit. Behind her, the door opened. Lifting her head, she turned slightly and smiled at Caleb.

"So, this is snow," he commented. "I think I knew that."

"This is snow," she agreed, tilting her chin to once again take in the extraordinary beauty of the day. "That stuff the night before last was just a tease. Thank you, by the way, for sweeping the porch."

For several seconds, Caleb stared at her in silence. "What do you mean?"

Meg clutched the shawl tighter in front of her throat, her gaze scanning the porch as a feeling of dread stole over her. Her heart thudded and kicked into high gear. On the small table beneath the window, a vase held paper flowers made from tissue. Closing her eyes, Meg swayed on her feet.

"No," she said, returning her hands to her face. "Oh, God," she cried, pushing past Caleb to get back inside the house. He followed her in, swinging the door shut, watching with his forehead creased in concern. Meg paced to the counter and back, coming to a halt before him.

"This isn't happening. It can't be."

"What isn't happening, Meg?"

"This," she stated with an expansive gesture.

Caleb shook his head, took her hands, and clasped them in his. "Explain what you mean."

Staring down at the shape of his hands, so much larger than hers, Meg fought against panic. "We should sit down," she said.

At the table, he pulled out a chair for her and another for himself. He sat facing her, knee to knee. Meg thought of the soft-edged tissue flowers in the snow, the writing on the mirror, the countless other incidents she had attributed to him acting out her recollection of events.

Breathing shallowly, Meg took his hand. She could hardly look at him. "I'm hoping," she began, "that you are doing things you don't realize you're doing, that you don't remember doing."

He tipped his head a little to the side, regarding her with a quiet speculation. "Like what?"

"Have you come into the bathroom while I've been showering and drawn in the steam on the mirror?"

Startled, he considered for a moment. "No," he said. She could tell by his expression he firmly believed he hadn't, and her question confused him. She inhaled, expanding her lungs, releasing the breath to try again. "Did you sweep the porch clean of snow?"

"No. Are you saying I did it and don't recall?" he asked after a moment.

"Worse. Right now, there's a vase out there on the porch on the table by the window with paper flowers in it."

"Paper flowers?"

"Yes. The first year Matt and I were married, he made me flowers out of bathroom tissue to commemorate our first snowfall as a married couple. And the other morning, when I was in the shower, I came out and found something I'd thought you had drawn on the steamed-up mirror."

"I had drawn something on the mirror," he repeated, as if for clarification.

"Yes," she said, leaning forward in her urgency. "Yes! I thought it had to be you, don't you see? Even though these are things Matt had done in the past, I thought you were doing them now."

Caleb's shoulders shifted and resettled, his elbows on his thighs, her hand in his. He didn't move, thinking for a moment before lifting his head to look at her. "Meg, there's another explanation. You know there is."

Meg stared into eyes the color of the murky sea. Her chest tightened. "I just... Matt's not in the country. Agent Phillips said—"

"You told me they lost track of him nearly two months ago," Caleb interrupted her. "He could be anywhere. Even here."

Even here.

Meg stood, dropping Caleb's hands. She could feel herself shaking, as if it might be someone else's body. The quivering started in her abdomen and worked its way out to her extremities. Lifting her fingers to her forehead, she could see them quaking, too, but could do nothing to make them stop until she clenched her hand into a fist and pressed it tight against the curve of her brow.

"That would mean he's been in the house," she said, her voice thick in her throat. "While we have been here, you and I, and we didn't know it."

Tucking her hands beneath her arms, Meg stared at the red and white tea towel hanging on the handle to the oven. She looked at how it had been folded, remembering a half dozen times in the past week when she had lifted the towel to spread the fabric out across the handle, thinking irritably it would never dry folded the way she'd found it. Not blaming anyone, not even giving the matter much thought, just an automatic action, old habit, but she remembered now who used to leave the dish towels like that every time he used one. "Oh, my God, even this."

"Even what?"

"The dish towel. We used to argue about it. Stupid thing to argue about. I spread it to dry and he...he always folded it. Like that."

She gasped, feeling a sudden lack of oxygen, and spun around, clutching the counter at her back for support. Staring at the floor, she tried to focus, to stop the linoleum from tilting beneath her feet. If Matt had come anywhere near here, knowing himself a hunted man, there had to be a reason he would take that risk. The reason couldn't be her. Not her, after all this time.

Shaking her head, she hurried to the refrigerator and yanked down the card she'd attached to the steel front with a magnet. She should call the number on the card Agent Phillips had left with her, shouldn't she? But then, they would find Caleb. Would that be so bad? To him, it would. He wasn't ready for questions, and she knew he wasn't.

"Meg!"

She hadn't realized she'd begun pacing in circles until he stopped her. Taking her by the upper arms, Caleb gave her a sharp shake. Her head snapped back on her shoulders.

"Look at me, Meg. Look at me."

Crazed, frightened, nearly blind with a number of emotions she couldn't name, Meg lifted her gaze to Caleb's, seeking his steadiness. "I'm looking," she said.

"Good. Now I want you to calm down, okay? Can you do that?"

Meg nodded.

"Perfect. I need you to be truthful with me. Is there any possibility he might be dangerous?"

She blinked. "To you?"

"To you, to me," he said. "It doesn't matter. What I'm asking is if we should be worried that he's here. Because he is. You know he is. Somewhere around, able to gain access when he chooses."

Alarm pounded through her skull along with a vivid flash of memory, of her cheek striking the wooden floor of the bedroom, the reek of stale whiskey in her nostrils, the metallic taste of blood filling her mouth, slurred, angered words over her head. "Maybe," she said.

His respiration caught and something new moved behind Caleb's eyes. He saw it, too. Her memory. It was *her* memory behind those lids.

Caleb straightened his shoulders, reaction stiffening his spine. He put his hand on the side of her neck, the warm, calloused ridges of his thumb behind her jaw pressing lightly against the rapid pulse of her blood. His expression altered, hardened. "There has to be a plan, Meg. We'll check the property first. The outbuilding, underneath the porch, anywhere he might conceivably be or have hidden. After that, we check the house, thoroughly. We keep the doors locked at all times. That way if he wants to come in again, he breaks in, and we know it."

Meg nodded, further calmed by his decisiveness. Somewhere in the life he'd known, Caleb Hunter had been an aggressively capable man. He still was. Nothing in the uncommon situation these past weeks had truly shaken him.

"What about the police, the FBI?" she asked him. "Interpol?"

"Not yet," he said. "If necessary, I will have to deal with them, I know. The question for you is—do you want Matt apprehended?"

Meg hesitated. "I…I don't know."

Releasing her neck, Caleb pushed her hair back behind her ear. "Then leave them out of it for now. We don't know for certain he's still close by."

"He was right out there a short time ago," Meg reminded him, nodding toward the porch. He grunted in acceptance. "I think," Meg said, "that what we're doing might be construed as harboring a fugitive or, at the least, obstruction of justice."

Caleb made another noise in his throat, shaking his head. "We're not harboring. We're not obstructing. We are securing the sanctity of your home." He seemed as surprised as she by the fierce tone of his statement and took a step away.

"They might already have some idea he's in the area, which would go a long way in explaining the coincidence of them coming to speak with you when you started noticing these occurrences," he said. "Let me get my coat back on. We'll lock the house as we leave it and check outside."

He started across the floor, stopping half a dozen feet away to pivot on his heel. "These things he's done, that you thought I had done, seem personal, something more than a way to alert you to his presence. What do you think his point is?"

Cruelty, she wanted to say, because in the end Matt had displayed a cruel streak in his dealings with her. But she couldn't be sure anymore of his motivation. Looking at the man before her, a man transformed in some manner by this call to action, she realized she couldn't be sure of anything.

Chapter 17

Caleb had secured all doors and windows in such a fashion that any entry whatsoever would be known. A simple matter, really, to create a network of security with only items at hand, like wire and duct tape, old keys, and empty tin cans. He surprised himself with the knowledge that had come to him, understanding that he had started to remember something...but what? He shrugged it off. If he couldn't grasp the answer easily, there seemed little point in delving. All he would get for his efforts would be a recurrence of the headaches that had plagued him those first few days after he had woken up on the beach, and he didn't need the distraction.

Standing in the darkness of the bedroom, Caleb listened to the gentle sound of Meg's breathing, a woman so trusting he was sometimes frightened for her. She had no clue who or what he might be, yet she had opened her home, her life, and herself to him. He had taken what she offered willingly. It didn't seem he could refuse.

He crossed the floor and kneeled beside the bed, turning his head so he aligned his face with hers. He looked at the color of her hair in the night, the shape of her eyelids, her forehead, the slight bump in the otherwise straight line of her nose, the curve of her mouth. He pressed his lips to the arch of an eyebrow and sat back over his heels, watching to see if she would awaken. She didn't.

Too trusting, he thought, and stood up.

He'd fallen in love with her, he understood he had, but he couldn't be sure if the love was for Meg's sake or was the transference of an emotion he held for another in his life. Sometimes, he thought it might be the latter because the love would occasionally startle him by not seeming new, as if it had been years in creation.

What did it matter? When he regained his memory, everything could change. All these moments he found himself treasuring might eventually mean little to him when he no longer needed their security. He would find himself walking away, not looking back, because he had to. Right?

Wrong. Fucking wrong. That had to be wrong.

Moving to the window, he slid aside the curtain, lifted the shade, and stared out into the night. The moon rode nearly half full in the sky, its white light shimmering on the sand, the roadway, on the glint of glass beneath the pine trees. Caleb narrowed his eyes, trying to focus on the tiny pinpoint of light. He had seen evidence of something there before more than once. Could Matt Donovan be waiting in a vehicle in the darkness for the right moment to enter the home that once had been his?

As Caleb looked across the moonlit stretch of road, a certain darkness moved within him, nearly choked him, and he stepped back, letting the curtain fall. Anger wouldn't help him or Meg right now. He could go out there and confront the man, but if it wasn't Donovan, both Meg and the house would be unprotected. Exhaling, he went back to the bed and sat down on the edge of the mattress in the vacant place left by the curve of Meg's body. She rolled toward him as the mattress sagged beneath his weight. He caught her by the arm.

"What is it, Caleb?" she mumbled sleepily.

"Nothing," he said.

"Why are you awake?"

I haven't slept in days, he thought. *Haven't you noticed?*

He needed sleep. Not only had his temper grown short, but he'd also found himself becoming physically unsteady. He hadn't made love to Meg since the day she'd found out the truth about her un-dead husband. Well, he needed to, now. Wanted to make love to Meg with a sudden, fierce desire. To lose himself in her, to thrust a cock already growing hard into that place of tight, heated flesh. He wanted her arms around him, craved the sound of her cries. To hold her locked in his arms as she climaxed again and again, knowing he, and no one else, brought her there. He wanted to make her forget there had ever been another man in her life, another man who hurt her, made her grieve, who left her and died away from her, only to come back to life and into her heart again, unwanted and unlooked for.

God, he needed to sleep, he badly needed to sleep, but he couldn't. Who would watch over her if he slept?

"Caleb, lie down."

How do you keep doing that, Meg? Get out of my head!

Groaning, Caleb clutched his brow. His head spun, his stomach churned. Reeling, he stood up, but she dragged him back down, her two hands clinging to the back of his shirt.

"Caleb, you need to sleep. Lie down."

Scrambling into a seated position, she worked his shirt over his head and unzipped his jeans, then pushed him onto the mattress and yanked them off. With remarkable strength, when he knew he couldn't possibly be any help at all, she shoved him around until she had him under the blankets.

"Close your eyes."

"I can't."

"You have to."

"I can't."

She drew a sharp breath. He saw the glitter of her green, green eyes in the darkness.

"Then do something conducive to relaxation, Caleb."

"What? Fucking?"

She narrowed her eyes at his rudeness, but she didn't say anything in condemnation. Instead, she got up on her knees and yanked off her sweatshirt. Her breasts gleamed in the darkness, heavy and milky white. Chilled, her nipples stood erect. She leaned toward him.

"If that's what you want to call it, fine," she whispered. "You'll sleep afterward, I promise you."

Reaching up he caught a breast in his hand and pulled her closer, then worked his tongue in slow circles around the rosy areola, lightly clamping his teeth on the tip, licking her nipple with the blunted edge of his tongue until she started to moan. Blood rushed headlong to his groin. Slipping his other hand into her flannel pajama bottoms, he stroked the moist flesh between her legs, finding her soaked and ready for him.

"Take those pajamas off." And all he could think was that he wanted to drive the image of Matt Donovan right from her head. "Come here. Right here."

Either she hadn't seen his gesture in the dark, or she pretended to misunderstand. He cupped his hands along the inside of her thighs and pulled her to the place he wanted her. With a silent shudder of anticipation, she leaned her arms against the wall above his head.

"You're going to come as soon as I put my mouth on you," he said.

"You're pretty darn sure of yourself."

"Yeah," he said, "I am."

With good reason. Nothing could have held her back. No sooner had he run his tongue along her slick flesh and circled the swollen bud of her clitoris and she was done, a scream of pleasure filling his ears. Wanting more, he captured her with his hands, held her in place on the mattress, bringing her to climax yet again, both of them shaking, skin shining with sweat even in the chill of the room. And when he mounted her and drove himself deep for forgetfulness and lust, for comfort, for love, it was his name she called.

His name.

Curled against him beneath the mounded quilt and blankets, she promptly fell asleep in his arms. "You don't love him, do you?" Caleb asked in the safety of her slumber, when he knew her dreams were not of a husband who had abandoned her, and she wouldn't wake to answer anyway.

* * * *

Two hours later, he woke as if someone had shouted in his ear. He could almost hear the reverberation of the words *damn you to hell* shattering the quiet night. For a moment, he thought Meg had cried out in her sleep, but she slept soundly, her head on her arm and the blankets tangled around her waist. With care, he freed the quilt and pulled it up over her shoulders before he got out of bed.

Naked, he shivered in the darkness, wide awake, alert to the night around him, straining for the sound of anything to indicate they were not alone in the house. Reaching up, he fingered the place on the back of his skull where the knot had been. Though Meg assured him the bruising had long since yellowed and faded away, he still had tenderness there. Tonight, the bone throbbed.

Snatching his clothes from the bottom of the bed, he thrust his legs into his pants and pulled the shirt on. Time, he mused without humor, to check the defenses.

Caleb made his way through the house in near silence, not bothering to turn on any lights as he went. No need to alert Matt to his actions, to light his way to Caleb or to an escape. Caleb's eyes had grown used to the darkness, his body to the places he needed to be where he would not betray his presence. He thought, briefly, of the men who had tried to kill him and the threat he had anticipated that had not yet come.

Deal with one threat at a time, Caleb Hunter, he reminded himself.

Matt Donovan's little love notes were not what they appeared to be. To Caleb, they appeared menacing in the extreme. Screw what he could and couldn't remember. He knew a decent man didn't break into the home of the wife he'd walked away from, leaving behind reminders of a life they no longer shared as the sole indicator of his presence. Did Matt hope for a sweet little reunion? Over Caleb's dead body, if it were true, but he knew it wasn't. Whatever Matt intended, it was nothing sweet.

He continued through the house, checking the attic door, the basement door, all the exterior doors and windows, the simple but effective devices he had set up to give warning of entry or an attempt at entry. All appeared to be in order.

Releasing a breath, permitting his shoulders to relax, he turned on the light over the stove in the kitchen and filled a pot with water, then set it on the stove to heat. A cup of that tea Meg liked...what was it called? Chamomile. A cup of chamomile tea might settle him down to the point where he could sleep again. She swore by it. That and warm milk. His first night in the house she had made him a cup of warm milk to help him sleep.

He remembered, too, that scalding his mouth reminded Meg of her husband, who used to do the same thing.

Shit.

With a flick of his wrist, Caleb turned off the burner. He didn't want anything he did to remind her of Matt. Not anything.

Lifting his eyes from the knob on the stove, he spotted the mug on the counter and reached to put it away. Fingers hovering in the air above the receptacle, he realized he hadn't taken one out of the cabinet. A spoon lay beside it. Bending closer, he saw what looked like a skim of overheated milk clinging to the concave metal. The mug held its own residue of whitish liquid. In the two hours he'd been asleep, Meg had not moved from the bed, he would swear to that, and he had been the last one to climb the stairs. The kitchen had been neat and orderly when they'd retired, the way Meg liked to leave it before she went upstairs for the night.

Stepping away from the stove, Caleb's gaze swept the kitchen. Everything else appeared as it had been the last time he passed through, except...the dish towel on the handle of the oven, bunched and folded over on itself. Caleb took another step away, his heart rate increasing in thudding increments. He backed up against the table, the legs sliding a bit across the floor, and he spun to keep the noise from waking Meg. He opened his hand across the scarred wooden surface. His first day here he'd noted the scratches on the top, a word he couldn't read and hadn't bothered to try in the days after. He saw it now, though, not one word but several, deeply etched into the wood. Where before the edges had been soft and worn from countless scrubbing, they were now raw and jagged. Lunging forward, he leaned above the fresh markings scored over the old.

I had to leave you, it read, had always read, and next to it further scribed in the same hand by a wickedly sharp instrument, *but now I'm back.*

Caleb straightened with a harsh invective. What kind of game was this bastard playing? And how the hell had he gotten in?

There was only one possibility. He'd been here all along, hiding in some location they hadn't discovered. Caleb stared at the cabinets, wondering if they could hold a man undetected. Grabbing the heavy flashlight Meg kept on the shelf, he spun it around in his hand like a weapon and rushed to the lower doors. He yanked them open one by one, half expecting to find Matt Donovan twisted like a contortionist around the pots and pans. Not surprisingly, he found nothing. No use bothering with the upper cabinets. They would never support a man's weight.

The pantry checked out clear, as did the area behind the door near the porch where he had found Donovan's jacket hanging, as if Meg had expected him to walk back in one day in need of the garment. Moving into the hallway, he began to systematically recheck each room, every piece of furniture with a door, every corner blocked from view.

"Come on," he ground out between his teeth. "Show yourself."

Nothing.

Nothing anywhere.

Fuck.

In the room Meg used as a studio, Caleb turned on the overhead light. The room held multiple cabinets where she stored her paints and brushes, cleaners, canvas, and various types and sizes of paper. He yanked open the door to each without result. Breathing heavily in the middle of the floor, Caleb spun in a slow circle, making certain he hadn't missed anything. Then he saw the painting.

When had she started working on that again? The sea looked more menacing than ever, the colors darker, the movement of the waves altered somehow to be more ominous and powerful. He moved closer. The debris she had painted bearing the name of Donovan's vessel was still there, tossed about by the fury of the ocean. The sky above looked bruised and embattled. And there, what was that? It looked like—

Caleb jerked away. For the love of God, it looked like a man's face beneath the surface, wide-eyed in horror as he sank out of sight, the visage barely discernible to the point where Caleb thought for certain he had imagined it until he looked again.

"Oh, God, Meg," he whispered. How could someone who painted those lovely illustrations filling the books on the living room shelf be capable of this darkness of vision? What haunted her that she had returned to this painting? Her husband. Matt Donovan haunted her. In life, not in death.

Caleb backed out of the room, not wanting to turn his back on the painting. With the flat of his palm, he smacked the light switch down and pulled the door shut.

After climbing the stairs, Caleb searched the rooms on the upper storey with the same diligence he had given the downstairs. The bathroom, the guest room, the third bedroom, which held nothing but an old desk and some boxes. He paused at the attic door. Determined, he removed the wire he had set up as a trip to indicate if the door had been opened. He didn't know how it could have been done, but if any possibility of hiding without detection existed, the attic would be the place.

Caleb flipped the switch just inside the door, turning on the bare bulb hanging from the rafters at the top of the stairwell. Shadows leaped into existence. Golden light limned each step. After listening for sounds of movement, Caleb ascended.

The dust on the floor had been disturbed when he and Meg had searched previously, but he found nothing there to alert him to fresh disruption. Utilizing the flashlight to illuminate the shadows he cast as he passed in front of the hanging fixture, Caleb scanned the large area quickly before beginning a more thorough search. Yanking boxes away from the wall, he checked behind them. He shoved outdated clothes around inside the old armoire, peering through fabric, prodding past jackets and dresses. He'd checked all these places with Meg already, but apprehension compelled him to look again. His nerves stretched and tightened. If Donovan wasn't here, then where the hell was he?

Cobwebs drifted in an unseen current, catching in his hair. He brushed them aside. The attic was cold, unheated. If Donovan hid there, he wouldn't find the accommodation comfortable. Caleb continued in his search, opening cardboard boxes large enough to contain a man, shining the flashlight under the eaves where a man might lay prone, unseen. Old canvases against the wall shielded an area about eight feet square. Plenty of room, and the leaning pile of stretched canvases, some of the paintings partially stripped of pigment, would provide insulation against the cold. A stab of unease chilled Caleb's flesh beneath his clothes. He walked closer, lifting the light in his hand as the hair along his forearms stood straight. The concentrated beam of the flashlight penetrated deep into the cavern of canvas to pass across a pair of brown eyes.

Swearing, Caleb rushed forward with the flashlight raised in his fist. He flung aside the framed canvases, stopping dead with sweat popping out on his forehead, his arms, the indentation above his upper lip when he saw himself against the wall. Dropping to his knees, he reached out to pull the painting forward. A portrait signed by Meg and dated more than eight months prior.

His stomach clenched and he swallowed hard to prevent the spillage of bile and his evening meal right there on the attic floor.

Meg had lied. She knew him.

Chapter 18

Dan wadded up the oily wrapper from the sandwich he'd eaten and tossed it into the bag on the car floor between Dutch Phillips' legs. Andre, the guy from Interpol, grunted and lobbed his own trash toward the bag and missed. The paper bounced and landed on the mat.

Dan unscrewed the cap from his soda and took a long pull. Beside him, Phillips held a pair of binoculars trained on the house. Only a few minutes earlier, the FBI agent had dubbed him dedicated, said he never would have expected a local to be donating his free time to an investigation. Obviously, Phillips didn't know how long he'd been investigating without any sanction from the powers that be. Frankly, Dan was grateful for the company. After the last time, he hadn't been too keen on sitting anywhere near Meg's house alone. Even though common sense told him what he'd seen had been a result of stress and too little sleep, he still got an uneasy feeling whenever he thought about it. A heart attack from stress was more likely than death by fright. Common sense. Anyway, he hadn't suffered any heart attack. The tests had proved it. Still, he didn't care to look too long at that stretch of beach behind her place.

In the backseat, Andre sighed. Dan heard him shifting, stretching out his legs.

"Can you tell me again why you expect our guy might show up here? Didn't he walk out on his wife years ago?" Andre asked.

"Why wouldn't he?" Phillips tossed back. "Last word we had, from your associate I might remind you, was that he was heading back to the States. Figure this is as good a place to start checking as any. Not only that, but did you see how she shut the door to the stairs when we went in the kitchen the other day? I don't think she was hiding a pile of dirty laundry on the steps."

"We should have asked to have a look around," Andre grumbled.

"On what grounds? We were there only to have her identify the subjects in the photographs."

Dan screwed the cap back on his soda and pegged the bottle into the cup holder. "I think you're wrong about Donovan being here. If he's smart, he'll stay away. Wouldn't this be the first place you'd look? Besides, the guy who's been camped out with her for the past couple of weeks doesn't look like the type to take the return of her ex lying down."

Phillips lowered the binoculars a fraction, cutting his eyes in Dan's direction. "What did you say his name is?"

"I didn't, and I don't know. I only met him once, with her in town, and we weren't introduced."

He remembered that day clearly. He had seen her go into the drugstore and had held back a minute or so before following her in, glancing at her boyfriend in the car as he passed. Dan had been jealous as hell when he'd gotten inside and had seen her purchase. That unexpected emotion had made him sarcastic when he had really needed her to speak with him. Not only to discuss what he'd found on the beach, but also about what came after. He didn't think she'd experienced anything similar—God, he hoped not—but he had needed to talk to someone about it, and she seemed, somehow, the most likely ear. Well, fat chance of that with lover boy sitting in the car waiting for her.

He remembered, too, the way Meg had closed her eyes when he tried to get her to listen to him, as if she could shut him out, and then her boyfriend had turned his head. Nothing could have prepared Dan for the expression on the guy's face. Dan didn't consider himself a timid individual, but he had actually shivered when greeted by the cold, menacing aspect of those eyes. He hoped Meg wasn't getting in over her head, mixing up with more trouble. He'd seen that same look on Matt Donovan's face on more than one occasion. Flat. Hard. Most of the time, that fisherman could be as cordial as any other resident in this town, but when crossed, he became something else entirely.

After Matt had left Meg and headed north—not far enough north, as far as Dan was concerned—the tales of his exploits were commonly spoken of among Matt's old mates. Drug running. Cargo stolen off the docks and sold to the highest bidder. Indiscriminate and vicious fights that left men battered, occasionally hospitalized, as if the rage that had occasionally shown itself when he and Matt were kids had somehow taken him over. It was difficult to remember the circumstance of their friendship, his and Matt's, in grade school. By high school, they'd parted ways. Even so, during Dan's investigation, Matt had relied on their early relationship to protect him from real scrutiny. Matt had been plenty pissed when it hadn't.

Still, Dan had never been able to obtain enough solid evidence. He'd tried. Yeah, he'd tried for a long time. And then word had come that Matt's ship had gone down. How the hell had the guy pulled that off?

"You sound like that might be bothering you a bit," Phillips said.

"What's that?" Dan asked, feeling a slight heat worm into his skin. Even though he knew what Phillips meant, he refused to rise to the bait.

In the backseat, Andre leaned forward again, interested. "You have a thing for Ms. Donovan?"

"What?" countered Dan, trying to sound casual. "Don't tell me you didn't notice she's a good-looking woman?"

"Very pretty," Andre agreed, but Phillips remained mute.

"Well then," said Dan, hoping to dismiss the subject.

Dutch Phillips lowered the binoculars again, setting them on his thigh. "Nice breasts."

Dan's stomach muscles clenched. He knew Phillips had passed the comment deliberately to see how he would react. Did Phillips think he might be biased? Was he testing him? Fine.

"Very nice breasts," Dan said and laughed as if the whole conversation was a joke. Until he remembered the last time he had been sitting in this exact spot, the night he ended up in the hospital. Before he'd gone onto the beach and had his run-in with that *thing*—had it possibly been a ghost, after all?—he'd had his own glasses trained on the kitchen window, watching Meg's new boyfriend putting his mouth all over those breasts. The muscle in his jaw tightened, teeth grinding together.

"What's up there?" Andre asked suddenly. "Attic?"

A narrow rectangle of light had appeared at the top of the house. "Probably," said Phillips. "Stauffer, do you know?"

"I've never been up there, but I would suppose it's an attic, yes," he stated flatly. He reached for his field glasses and fitted them against his eyes, focusing on the window. "What time is it?"

From the corner of his eye, he saw a brief flash of green as Andre pressed the watch on his wrist to illuminate it.

"Three-seventeen."

"Odd time to be rooting through your attic," Phillips commented.

Dan said nothing. He hadn't been able to put his finger on what had been bothering him since they'd begun the surveillance, but he suddenly realized the reason for his disturbance. Meg was fairly careless about her windows—hence the little peep show the evening he'd found the debris from Donovan's boat—but tonight every shade, every blind had been drawn down tight. Did she and her boyfriend know he and the two agents were out here?

Through the bare attic window, Dan could see what appeared to be the illumination of a naked bulb, the crisscrossed shadows pierced by brighter flashes flicking back and forth.

"Flashlight," said Phillips after a couple more minutes, giving voice to the conclusion he'd already drawn.

"Could it be our man?" asked the agent in the backseat.

"We didn't see anyone go in," Dan reminded Andre.

"He wouldn't be likely to use the front door. But it could be like I said—she's been hiding him here the whole time."

"No," said Dan. "No way."

"What makes you so certain?"

What made him certain? The fact he remembered how she'd reacted when he'd brought word her husband had died. She'd been shocked, yes, and grief stricken, too, but relieved. The guilt of her relief had crushed her. He knew it had. Her guilt, more than her mourning, had kept her solitary for so long.

"What the hell is that?"

A flurry of shadowed motion reflected on the glass and then, as he and Phillips watched and Andre scrambled to find what they were looking at with his naked eye, a darkness bloomed in the yellow illumination inside the attic, blocking out the light. Remembered dread and fear crawled over Dan's skin, making his breath come short. Beside him, the FBI agent seemed merely interested. Damn it, hadn't he seen that?

The black shape of a man—and yet not like any man Dan had encountered outside of a nightmare—continued to grow until no light remained in the space beneath the steeply pitched roof. Dan choked, recalling again those long minutes in the car as he waited for the ambulance to arrive, fearing whatever he'd seen on the beach would hunt him down. He hadn't imagined the episode, not from stress or lack of sleep. What he'd seen had been real. But what the fuck had it been? What was it now, overwhelming the light in Meg's attic?

The shadow with its overpowering sense of evil vanished, and Dan could breathe again. The other two men started exchanging theories about what the fellow in the attic had been tossing around. Paintings, they concluded.

Paintings? No freaking way. Hadn't they *seen*?

Chapter 19

"Meg, explain this to me. Please."

At the desperate tone of Caleb's voice in the darkness, Meg came wide awake, tossing back the blanket to sit up against the headboard. She switched the light on, then sat squinting at Caleb in the doorway. He held up a canvas with both hands before him.

"Where'd you get that? Were you up in the attic?" she asked, disoriented. She hadn't heard a thing, but now she could hear the slamming of her heart in her chest. "What's going on?"

"Explain this to me," he said again.

Rubbing her eyes, Meg reached for the clothes she'd discarded earlier and put them on before climbing out of bed. Placing her fingers on the edge of the stretched canvas frame, she lifted the painting away from Caleb and leaned the portrait against the wall. Crossing her arms, she took several steps back, frowning at the painting.

"I painted that shortly after I heard Matt's ship had gone down," she said, spinning on her bare heel to face Caleb. The look on his face made her flinch away.

"Go on," he said.

"Then I didn't want it around, so I put it in the attic." Simply stated but the truth. Or all she meant to tell of it at this hour.

"How did you paint that?" demanded Caleb. "Another one of your dreams?"

If he had uttered the words differently, she would have thought them sarcastic. She didn't understand what he meant or why he asked.

"No," she said. "I had photographs."

"Of me."

"Of you?"

He darted past her to point at her signature and the date at the bottom of the portrait. "Yes, of me! Is that how you're going to explain it? That you painted this picture of me before we'd met from a photograph? What were you doing with a photograph of me? You know me. You lied and you know me. Tell me who I am, Meg! Tell me."

Grabbing her arm, he pulled her closer to the painting. Yet even in his agitation, his fingers circled her upper arm without aggression. Her racing heart began to slow its pace. Caleb wasn't Matt with his latent violent tendencies. She didn't need to be wary of him.

Tilting her head to the side, Meg studied the portrait. She hadn't looked at it for more than half a year. Freeing her arm of his grasp, she crouched down on the floor.

"That's not you," she said, frowning as she tried to ascertain the resemblance that might have confused him. "That's Matt."

He didn't even pause to consider her words. "You lied when you said you didn't know me, and you're lying still."

Glancing up at him, she shook her head. "No, Caleb, I'm not. Look. Look at the painting." She reached out to touch him in reassurance. He drew away.

"I thought you were the one who is too trusting. I'm a fool," he whispered.

His words struck her in the heart. She flinched in pain.

Standing up, she crossed her arms to hug herself. Poor Caleb. What did he see when he looked at Matt's portrait? Obviously, not what she saw. His emotional state, the fact he hadn't been sleeping well for the past several days, on guard, on edge, feeling this need to protect her could account for his sudden distrust, his confusion. The portrait had never been meant to be a true-to-life portrayal but had developed from what she'd been feeling at the time. Not abstract, by any means, but more of a caricatured interpretation. Features exaggerated, emphasized, while others were a mere wash of color, a hint. Granted, Matt and Caleb had similar dark hair. Because he had never known Matt or what he looked like, she could see why Caleb might be bewildered.

"I can show you the photographs I used," she suggested. "Would that help?"

After a moment, he relented. "Yes," he said.

Crossing the floor, Meg yanked open a drawer in the low dresser beneath the window, then reached in for the photo album. Shoving aside paperwork, articles from magazines, odds and ends of items better off in the trash, she found the thick album of photographs gone. Her extended fingers clenched into a fist. "They're not here anymore."

"You're certain?"

Meg pivoted. "Yes," she said. Caleb turned away, his expression disbelieving as he bent to study the painting. Meg frowned at his back. Striding across the room, she grabbed the canvas with an angry sweep of her arm and marched it across the hall into the spare room where Caleb had spent the first couple of days. She tossed the portrait onto the bed, face down, and returned to her own room. Caleb still stood where she'd left him, his expression unsettled.

"Yes," she said again. "You haven't moved them, have you?"

"Of course not. I haven't looked at your things and wouldn't presume to take them, even if I had."

Of course not, Meg repeated to herself. "Matt, then," she said.

"Probably," Caleb agreed with an irksome calm.

Meg tried to remember the last time she had seen the album. She hadn't looked at it in months. "Damn it," she said beneath her breath. "When would he have taken it?"

"He was here tonight, Meg. I found evidence of him in the kitchen. That's why I went to the attic, looking for him. I don't know how he's getting in and out. I thought I had devised a system that would work, to let us know if he came in, but I failed. I'm failing. I can't keep you safe, Meg."

A shiver ran down her back at his words. "Why do you believe you need to keep me safe?"

"He hurt you. I know that he did."

Meg closed her eyes. Oh, yes, he had hurt her. She hadn't wanted to think about that, to remember those times when her husband had seemed like another sort of creature entirely, violent and cold and without reason. He had been another man then, one she didn't know. But she had held out hope he loved her still. Stupid and unrealistic, but perhaps the fate of the abused.

"It's not your responsibility to keep me safe," she said softly. "And you're not failing. You're diligent. Too diligent. You're going to kill yourself from exhaustion. Maybe it's time we called the authorities. I know you don't want to. I understand your reasons. But something has to be done."

His shoulders slumping, his head dropped forward. He looked tired to the point of being gray. "I don't know," he said on a weary exhale.

Meg stalked to the door and crossed the hall one more time, removing the chair from the guest room. Returning with it, she closed the bedroom door and turned the lock, shoving the sturdy back of the chair beneath the door handle. At Caleb's quizzical look, she said, "It works in the movies," and yanked down the covers of the bed, pointing at the rumpled sheets. "Lie down," she ordered. "It's my turn to keep watch."

"No—"

"Yes."

With a deep breath, he relented, lying down fully clothed. Meg pulled up the blankets and tucked them around his body. She touched his face, his jaw, smoothed the hair back from his brow. The gaze he turned her way softened, lost its look of desperation and suspicion.

"I would never lie to you, Caleb. I—" *love you*, she wanted to say but stopped herself. For one thing, love didn't preclude lying but often precipitated it. For another, saying the words aloud wouldn't mean they were true. It wouldn't mean Caleb would believe her or that he would want to hear those words from her. And the day could come when those words would stand between them, when he remembered his identity, his life, and found he had to leave her.

Meg placed her lips on his forehead until the furrow smoothed. "Good night," she whispered against his skin.

Turning off the light, she crossed to the other side of the bed and sat with her back against the headboard and her knees drawn up, displaying deliberate attentiveness. He had to be aware of her vigilance so he could relax.

His hand snaked across the mattress and slipped around hers. "Good night, Meg. I'm sorry if I frightened you about that portrait. I believe you. I know you wouldn't lie to me. I know that. I...I'm just so tired."

She squeezed his fingers. "Go to sleep, then."

He pressed his forehead against her thigh, and she felt him nod. Letting go of his hand, she placed her fingers in his hair, stroking the thick, silky locks back across his crown several times before resting her hand atop the curve of his skull. In a few minutes, he fell asleep. Meg leaned her own head against the wall at her back, her shoulders pressed into the bars of the headboard. Deliberately, so the discomfort would keep her awake.

He had unnerved her in his insistence about the portrait. She feared his visual perception had suffered from the blow to his head. She should have insisted he go to a doctor.

God, he had been so upset, so despairing when he thought she had lied to him. Trust was a two-way street, as was honesty. Perhaps she should have told him more than she had about her life before, about Matt, about the things that had come between them.

Matt. Damn him. What did he think he was doing, coming back here? He'd walked out on her, walked out with absolutely no intention of returning, and then had created an entire scenario designed to lead everyone to believe the fishing boat had gone to rest somewhere at the bottom of the ocean. Apparently dealing in the smuggling of stolen goods—high-priced stolen goods, according to Agent Phillips—and possibly drugs was a lucrative enough occupation to make a man turn his back on everyone and everything he had known.

Meg's gaze drifted to the shut door, the chair wedged beneath the knob. She only hoped that trick worked. The fact Matt came and went at will, undetected, not making contact, leaving sadistic hints of a past long gone, made the hair slither to attention on the back of her neck. What did she and Caleb hope to accomplish riding this out on their own? Did they expect he would move on when he tired of his wicked games? Or that they would catch him in the act? Call the authorities and pray the commotion of his capture would enable Caleb to avoid too many questions? At first, she'd wished Matt would leave her alone, that she wouldn't have to deal with the responsibility of his arrest, but the more she thought about it, the more she just wanted it to end.

Remembering her vacillating emotions over the years made her angry, at herself more than anyone else. Protecting him, making excuses for him, trying to blame the breakup of her marriage on outside circumstances rather than the truth. The truth. So many truths existed, and not one of them came close to uncovering the final grimness of it all. Grief and relief had mingled as one when he'd died.

And now he hadn't.

Looking around the room, Meg thought of the past weeks with Caleb. She had allowed herself to lapse into a fantasy existence with this man who had washed up out of the dark tides of the sea. She'd been cocooned in the life she had fashioned with him, separated from the harsh realities of the world in a place of safety, special and tender.

Her gaze strayed once more to the chair jammed under the doorknob. She had known all along what she and Caleb had couldn't last in its pristine condition, but she'd never expected the house would come under attack, that this room would become a prison where she would have to lock herself away to avoid the one man she had thought she'd never see again.

Yet something inside of her wanted to see him, wanted one final chance to make right all that had gone wrong. *Oh, stop it!* Stop it.

"You're sick, you know that?" she muttered to herself.

To make it right. Not another chance at love with the man who had been her husband, but the chance for her to make it right, as if it would make her feel better about the demise of their relationship. How self-centered and stupid and self-righteous and delusional and...and any number of things. What had happened between the two of them had not been entirely her fault. Indeed, Matt's final slide into the dark life he'd chosen to lead had nothing to do with her at all.

Did it?

Meg closed her eyes, wanting nothing so badly than to go back in time, even four or five days, to the last night she and Caleb had spent together before the news of Matt's survival and his life of crime had been delivered. She longed to lie beside Caleb again in the darkness with everything between them both new and old and strangely, wonderfully perfect.

But that wouldn't happen. In the morning, they had some decisions to make.

Chapter 20

Meg shut the door and inserted the key into the lock. Caleb watched her perform the action, not believing for a moment the setting of a lock would do any good. They both had been missing something, something that would strike them as obvious when revealed, that would explain how Donovan had been getting into and out of the house without detection. As to the why of the man's actions, Meg had said only Donovan himself could explain the reason, and she meant to ask him as soon as he'd been apprehended.

Caleb had found Meg determined upon awakening, sharp-edged and fixed on a goal. She planned to take him into town, Meg to speak with the officer, Stauffer, and whoever else might be available and open for discussion, and Caleb, apparently, to lay his story out for a private investigator.

"Be honest with the guy," she'd said to him. "I don't know why I didn't think of it sooner, but this is what private investigators do. He's not going to make a report to the law, only to you."

Mulling over the particulars of how he would explain himself and his story, Caleb followed Meg to the car and got into the passenger's side. He smoothed the legs of his jeans down over his thighs and snapped the seatbelt into place. For the first time in days, the sun shone brightly. He lowered his lashes, glancing sidelong at Meg from beneath them as she started the engine.

She had pulled her hair into a loose ponytail at her nape, long bangs falling over her forehead and catching in her lashes when she blinked. Though pale and tired, she looked incredibly beautiful to him. Ethereally beautiful, like she might vanish at any moment. Her scarf hung loose around the collar of her coat, the fringe curling over her sleeve, the knit garment the same green as her eyes. He wanted to touch the fringe and her fingers, but he kept both of his hands firmly in his lap.

Abruptly, she reached into her purse and pulled out some paper bills. He frowned at their denomination, calculating in his head as she handed them to him. "What's this for?"

"To pay the investigator," she said. "He'll probably want a retainer, but this will have to do for now. Tell him you'll pay him to listen to you for an hour or so, and you'll determine afterward whether or not you want to hire him. That will buy me some time to get the funds together if he thinks he can help you."

"Meg," he said. "I can't have you paying for—"

"You have to. I'm not taking no for an answer. This needs to be done."

"You can come with me if you want."

"No, we agreed. My presence might inhibit you from being as honest as you need to be, and if I've ever actually shoved any of my thoughts into your head, I certainly don't want to be doing so during your discussion with the investigator."

He nodded, lifting his hips from the seat to shove the bills into his pocket. "I'll pay you back somehow," he said.

"You could do some work around the house," she told him, cutting her eyes to his. "In the springtime."

In the springtime, he repeated silently and smiled, feeling a bit of the tension leave his neck and shoulders.

The brief ride into town took place without further conversation. She poked her fingers into his hand and he held on, not releasing her until she needed to turn the wheel to pull into a parking space. She shoved the car into park, then leaned back against the seat.

"It'll be all right, Meg," he said.

"So you keep saying," she responded with a rueful turn of her lips.

"I mean it."

She turned her head, breath fogging the glass of the driver's side window, gaze on a couple walking side by side down the street. Caleb wondered if she knew them, wondered what it would be like for him to know anyone at all again besides Meg. She turned back, giving him a short nod as she yanked the keys from the ignition. "Let's go."

Cold air rushed in with the opening of the door. Meg climbed out, shut the door, and stepped up onto the curb before Caleb had moved. With reluctance, he followed and joined her on the sidewalk. He could smell the fragrance of her hair, freshly washed that morning in the shower while he had stood guard outside the bathroom door. Just in case.

"The investigator's office is about a block that way," she said with a jerk of her chin. She slipped her hand into his. "I'll walk to the door with you."

He experienced a rush of emotion at her offer, her determination to be with him until the moment when he must face the discussion of the vast unknown of his life with a stranger. The need to have her at his side pulled at him even then, but he knew he couldn't. Not for this.

Together they walked in the direction she'd indicated, hand in hand. The chill of an early winter day brightened her pale cheeks. He wanted to kiss her, hard, right there in the street.

"Tell him everything, Caleb," she said as she had earlier. "Everything you can think of."

He nodded, releasing her hand to hook an arm around her shoulder. She barely came up to his armpit. With a glitter like gold in the sun, her hair caught in the nap of his coat. From the moment he'd met her, he'd possessed this need to protect her. Maybe the difference in size, in physical stature, instilled in him the desire to keep her safe. But from what?

"Meg," he said quietly, "I don't want to leave you."

She sucked her lips in, pressing them together tightly as she drew a long breath through her nose and let it out.

"Maybe you won't have to," she said. "We don't know anything yet. You haven't remembered who you are, and even if this investigator helps you find out the details of your life, there might be nothing compelling you to go back to it. But if there is and you have to, if you want to go, then you must. I won't—I won't..." Her voice tapered off. Understanding, Caleb stopped walking and drew her close against his chest.

"If I must, then I'll miss you. I don't want to miss you."

She didn't say anything, but he heard her sniffling and knew she had started to cry. He pressed his mouth against her hair and held her until the small noise stopped. Her fingers moved back and forth across her face beneath her nose, her hand bumping against the front of his coat.

"Okay." She stepped back. "That's it. We're good. Whatever happens, we'll handle it. But right now we're where we need to be. And this is Craig Miner's office. You go on in, and I'll drive over to the police station and come back to get you in a bit."

He hesitated to turn up the short walkway to the glass door. Meg gave him a little push in the small of his back. "Go."

So he did.

He turned with a grip on the door handle to find her walking backward away from him. When she saw him turn, she raised her hand, then spun on her heel to hurry in the direction of her car, the green scarf drifting across the wool of her coat. She didn't look back. Maybe she couldn't. He went inside.

Blinking in the interior dimness, Caleb moved slowly to the desk where a pleasant-looking woman sat. She peered at him expectantly. "Yes?" she asked when he didn't speak.

"Caleb Hunter," he said after a quick clearing of his throat. "I'm here to see Craig Miner."

"Ah, yes. A young lady made that appointment, didn't she?"

Caleb nodded, not seeing why it mattered. Perhaps she wondered why the young lady in question hadn't come with him.

"Have a seat. Mr. Miner is with a client at the moment but should be finishing up shortly." She handed him a flat board with a clip on top that held a form of some sort and a pen. "Please fill out as much information on this sheet as is applicable."

Taking the items to the nearest chair, he sat with the board angled toward the light through the window.

Name. Okay, he knew the answer to that one. Address? Nope. Phone number? Meg's, he supposed. Birthdate? Social Security number? No idea. Reason for consult? It seemed too complicated to write down. He wouldn't know where to begin. Talking about the reasons would be more direct. Returning the pen to the clip, he set the board across his knee and waited, trying to relax. With a slight turn of his head, he could see the minimal traffic in the street, the sidewalk, brown leaves blown over the concrete surface by an abrupt breeze. In the shadowed corner of the window glass, he kept catching the edge of his reflection.

No matter what Meg thought, that portrait he'd found in the attic looked like him. She hadn't lied to him, but perhaps the psychic ability she kept talking about had somehow conveyed his image to her long before she had even dreamed him. Not that the portrait depicted anywhere near an exact likeness, but there had been enough of a resemblance to give him pause and make him doubt.

Spotting a small mirror on the wall across the waiting area, he stood up and walked over to the glass oval, then frowned at his reflection. He needed a haircut. Meg hadn't yet given him the trim she'd offered. He studied his face, the shape of his brow, his jaw, the earthy color of his eyes. Yes, enough of a resemblance, yet far from accurate. He could see the woman at the desk reflected in the mirror, watching him with curiosity, brow furrowed.

Caleb pivoted on his rubber heel. "Will Mr. Miner be a lot longer?"

"About fifteen minutes or so. I'd offer you a cup of coffee, but our maker broke. There's a shop across the street if you want to run and grab yourself a cup."

Depositing the form with its scanty information on the desk, Caleb decided that a cup of coffee might be a good way to kill the time. Crossing the street, Caleb glanced up and down the length, finding Meg's car already gone. Children played on the sidewalk not far away, and he saw people walking, driving by, and climbing in or out of parked cars. Though foreign, something about the town struck a chord of familiarity in his mind. Perhaps he'd come from some place similar, homey and slow-paced.

Yanking open the door to the Caffeine Café, Caleb went inside, the aroma of coffee strong, the scents varying and not entirely pleasant. A board behind the counter indicated the establishment offered a vast variety of coffee flavors, none of which sounded appealing to him.

"Plain coffee?" he asked.

"Okay, black coffee. What kind?"

"Just regular coffee," he said, "with milk and sugar. You have that?"

The boy shrugged, turning to pour him a cup of dark brew. "That'll be two dollars." Caleb reached into his pocket for one of the bills from Meg, watching carefully as the boy counted back the change.

Sitting down at a table by the window, he figured the woman in the investigator's office would see him and be able to get his attention if he didn't come back by the time Miner was ready to meet with him. The Caffeine Café offered other inducements besides coffee, with a section of the store filled with racks of magazines and books. A big, boxy contrivance in the corner with a curtained door had the words "Digital Photos" printed above it.

"What's that?" he asked the kid at the counter.

"What's what, man?"

"That in the corner."

"A photo booth. You go in, put in five bucks, and it takes your picture. Five of them. Gives 'em to you right away out that little slot at the side there."

Photographs would probably be a good thing to give the private investigator. He would be able to match them up to other pictures he might locate, perhaps in some sort of listing of people who were missing, if such a thing existed. Leaving his coffee on the table, Caleb went into the booth, then yanked the curtain shut across the door as instructed by the written placard in the device. Pulling the change he'd received from his pocket, he rifled through the paper money and plucked out a five dollar bill, which he inserted, face up, into the slot. Continuing to follow the instructions, he pushed the red button.

An immediate flash blinded him. As he brought his hands up in front of his eyes, another flash followed, then a third, a fourth, and a fifth, as he was trying to figure out what he should be doing.

"Crap, I've never felt so friggin' incapable in my life," he muttered and paused, holding his breath. That struck a chord like memory, an association between what was presently occurring and who he had been in the past. But he couldn't quite grasp the feeling as it slipped away.

Outside the machine, a whirring noise took place. He stuck his head out.

"Your pictures," said the boy at the counter. Seeing a strip of paper sticking out of the outside slot, Caleb grabbed it.

"Huh," he said. Couldn't see much of him in any of them. He had bent forward in the first one, held his hands up in the second and third, had bent forward again to look at the directions during the fourth, and was straightening back up when the fifth was taken. At least now, however, he had some idea how the machine worked. Fishing another five from his pocket, he decided to give the photo-taking thing another try.

Prepared when the flashes came this time, he kept his face directed toward the aperture in the wall. When the photographs popped out, he held them up to the light inside the booth. Sweat broke out across his forehead, cold as ice water. Reaching into his pocket, he pulled out the last five from his change. He slid the bill into the machine and drew the curtain closed again. A short time later, he yanked out the last set of prints and held these up to the light, as well.

"No."

* * * *

Meg stood in front of the police station, her heart beating rapidly, the flesh of her palms slick, reliving the anxiety of her question-and-answer sessions about Matt's activities. She and Matt had still been living under the same roof, sharing the same bed, and her fear of letting something slip that might condemn Matt had made her nauseous for days after. Still, Matt had blamed her for the interest of the police. He had accused her of telling them everything, even though she hadn't known anything, had no idea what the police had hoped to gain from their conversations with her. None of that mattered anymore.

She'd come to turn him in.

For several moments, she remained motionless on the sidewalk, the crushed shell in the tended beds to either side of the walkway white in the sun, ornamental grasses brown and blowing in the light breeze. So many times, she would have been justified in calling the police for Matt's behavior alone, but she had hoped she could shelter them both from consequences until they merely blew away like thistledown. In a way, she had been doing the same thing with Caleb. Time she learned from her mistakes.

Taking a deep breath, Meg marched up and through the doorway into the tiny lobby, halting in front of the window of bulletproof glass. "Yes?" asked the police clerk who had risen from behind her desk.

Meg leaned forward, projecting her voice closer to the concave opening below the bottom of the window. "I'm Meg Donovan. I've come to speak with Dan Stauffer. Is he here?" she added in afterthought.

"Hold on. Have a seat."

Too nervous to sit, she paced the small area. A frame on the wall held a group photo of the seven members on the force, including the clerk. Expression cocky despite the military stance, Dan stood just to the left of center, next to the now-retired chief. Many of the women in town liked that about Dan, his aggressive self-assurance. The day he'd shown up at her house with Agents Phillips and Andre, his confidence had been distinctly lacking.

The clerk returned, pushing open the door. Meg followed the young woman inside and down a side corridor off the main office. She knew exactly where they headed.

Claustrophobic by design, the interview room held a small table and a pair of chairs, the walls the same dark brick as the outside of the building. An overhead light shone down at just the right angle to annoy any person seated beneath. Nevertheless, Meg pushed a chair against the wall and sat so she would be facing the door when Dan came in. Two minutes later, he entered the room.

"Meg," he said.

"Dan," she answered. She pushed the other chair toward him with the side of her foot. He yanked the chair out, perching on the metal seat near the door he had closed behind him. Loosening her scarf and unbuttoning her coat, Meg stalled for time, searching for a way to begin. Despite her determination to have this conversation, she still didn't know where to start.

Folding her scarf on the table, she glanced at Dan. Beneath his bloodshot eyes, shadows smudged his skin.

"Are you all right?" she asked him.

"Do you care?"

The abrasive inappropriateness of his retort startled her. "You look tired."

He shrugged his shoulders. "What are you doing here?"

"I came to make a report. Should I be talking to you or to those other two men who were at the house?"

Reaching into the pocket of his shirt, he pulled out a pad and pen. "You can start with me. I'll put in a call when we're through and see if they want to question you, as well."

She cringed at the phrase "question you." Once again, it made her seem suspect. She straightened her spine against the chair back. "When the three of you came to show me those pictures, was there any other reason besides identification? Did you have reason to believe Matt was heading back here?"

"Why?" Dan shot at her. "Have you heard from him? Is he here?"

Though he attempted to act vaguely occupied with what she said by toying with the pen between his fingers and deliberately avoiding eye contact, she could tell by the shift of his shoulders she had caught his attention. "Yes," she said, dropping the single syllable between them with hardly a breath for air.

Dan clicked the tab at the top of his pen and looked up. "He's contacted you? You've seen him around? What?"

Meg leaned forward, twirling the fringe on the edge of her scarf. She bit her lip. "He's been in the house—"

"And your boyfriend didn't beat the crap out of him?"

Startled, Meg flinched. "Excuse me?"

"You know. The guy who couldn't buy his own rubbers."

He pronounced the last word like "rubbahs" in true New Englander fashion but drawn out and deliberate in a manner she'd never heard him use before. She frowned at him. "What?"

Dan shook his head irritably. "Never mind. Go on."

"No. What is your problem? I've come to you on official business and you're acting like the jilted suitor. I never even went out with you. You know that."

"Yeah, I know that," he said, tossing the pen on the table. Sitting back, he folded his arms across his chest. "Go on. You've talked to Donovan, then?"

"I haven't talked to him," Meg continued, defensive. "I haven't seen him. Neither one of us has. But somehow he's gotten into the house and left indications he's been there, like a taunt."

Dan drew a deep breath, expanding the protective vest beneath his shirt. "How long has this been going on?"

"A few days," Meg said.

"A few days?" he echoed. "A few days? What the hell have you been waiting for?"

Tilting her chin, Meg stared at the finished brick of the wall above his head. "I don't know." With a sigh, she lowered her gaze to meet his light blue eyes dead on. His expression hardened. "I don't know," she repeated. "But I need your help, the help of someone in authority because it's not a good situation."

He watched her a few seconds before standing. Without speaking, he shoved his chair out of the way in order to open the door. Picking up her scarf from the table, Meg held it in her lap, burying her chilled fingers into the soft lamb's wool. When the door opened again five minutes later, the clerk from the front desk placed a Styrofoam cup down on the table in front of her and backed out of the room. Meg glanced at the drink. She didn't like her coffee black, but she put a hand around the cup, thinking it might warm her fingers. The insulating qualities of the container made short work of that notion. Meg shoved her hand back inside the scarf.

While she waited for Dan's return, Meg's thoughts turned again to Caleb, wondering how he fared with the private investigator. His lack of identity had become increasingly frustrating for him. She hoped Craig Miner could assist him. With any luck, he might convince Caleb of what she had wanted him to do all along: consult again with a doctor, submit to tests, both physical and psychological, and perhaps find his lost memories that way. Still, any facts discovered by the investigator might be enough to prompt recollection. Existing hand in hand with recollection, of course, was the probability that what she and Caleb shared could be lost. He had a life, another life, whole and entire, awaiting his return. They both knew that.

Meg closed her eyes.

Other factors had to be considered, as well. For his own safety, Caleb needed to remember who had tried to kill him. In all that had occurred over the past few days, she had nearly forgotten what had brought him to her. He seemed to have always been there.

She didn't think she should mention any of this to Dan unless she talked it over with Caleb first. Any decision would ultimately be his to make.

Glancing at the clock on the wall, she saw another ten minutes had passed. Steam no longer wafted from the coffee. Rising, Meg moved the handful of steps to the door and attempted to turn the knob. She sucked in a short gasp of air, reacting with the same claustrophobic intake of breath she'd experienced at finding the door locked during her series of interviews.

"Come on, Dan," she said to herself, returning to her seat. "Where are you?"

When next the door opened, three men filed in, filling the room to capacity. Dan and the fellow from Interpol stood against the wall, while Agent Phillips took the seat Dan had vacated. Phillips folded his hands on the table. Meg did not like the look on his face.

"Tell me what's been happening at your house," he said.

Meg considered the chronological order of events. She should have written it down. After a moment of silence, in which all three men stared at her intently, she told the story of the past few days. She understood by the few questions asked for clarification that the agents knew someone else had been living in her house. No doubt, Dan had mentioned Caleb's presence to these men.

"You shouldn't have waited so long to tell us this," Phillips said in a low voice.

"I know. And I know you're looking for him, which is why I'm here now. At least I am here now. And he didn't try to hurt...me," she finished, still attempting to steer clear of any reference to Caleb.

Agent Phillips shifted his hips on the hard seat and looked into her eyes. "He could have. Hurt you, I mean. We have come to believe he is responsible for the deaths of two of those men whose names are on the cross with his out on the point. They weren't willing to work with him, you see."

A chill coursed through her body in the space of a heartbeat, as if ice-cold blood had pumped into her veins. "I can't believe that."

"I'm afraid so. Certain agencies are still working on the details. So, you understand, he could have hurt you. Or worse. And there's something else, Mrs. Donovan."

She didn't want to know. But she didn't think she'd be able to prevent the words because Agent Phillips showed no inclination to close his mouth and walk back out the door.

"Go ahead," she whispered.

"I've said that he could have hurt you because there would have been that distinct possibility had he been at your home. That was where he was headed, our sources say. Hugging the coast in that ship of his, making his way up from the Caribbean."

Meg frowned. "What do you mean?"

Agent Phillips reached into the inside pocket of his suit coat and deposited an envelope on the table. "Whoever has been in your house," he said, opening the flap to spill the envelope's contents onto the laminate surface between them, "wasn't Matt Donovan. He's dead. Your husband is dead. His body was found washed up on the shore only a few miles from your house and identified by his fingerprints and dental records. We received word of the positive identification this morning. This time it's definite. He was killed sometime between three and five weeks ago. I'm sorry, Mrs. Donovan. I suppose I should say I'm sorry, shouldn't I? But you've thought for a long time now that he was gone, and I don't think you were hoping he'd come back."

Dead…again.

"H-how?" she stammered. Blindly, Meg reached for the photographs the agent had dumped on the table and pulled them toward her, some of them too gruesome to bear. But there were others. Oh, God, there were others…

"That answer is still part of an ongoing investigation, Mrs. Donovan. I can't give you the details now." He dropped his hand over the photos, sliding them away from her, choosing several from the pack to push back in her direction. She leaned her forearms on the table, gaping down at the black and white photographs.

Yes, the nearest one was Matt— dead, pale, battered, and lifeless. She'd never had the closure she needed the first time. She almost wished she didn't have it now. Her stomach flipped and twisted. She shuffled the photograph of her former husband back into the pile Agent Phillips held secured beneath his hand and looked at the other three, her heart pounding in her chest, nearly choking her. Pushing all but one of the photos away, she lurched to her feet, shoving her hand deep into the warmth of her scarf and grabbing her coat with the other. "I want to go home."

"Mrs. Donovan?"

"I want to go home," she repeated.

"Do you have anything else to say about what took place in your house these past several days?" Phillips asked in an offhand manner as he slipped the photos into the envelope. She could tell by the expressions exchanged between Phillips and Andre that they thought she had either fabricated the whole story or was a lunatic. Dan alone appeared to reserve judgment. She couldn't imagine why.

In the final analysis, what they thought of her didn't matter worth a damn. Only the truth mattered to her now, and to uncover the truth she had to retrieve Caleb and go home.

Chapter 21

Yanking open the door to the private investigator's office, Meg stepped into an empty waiting room. "Hello?" she called.

A middle-aged woman with burnt sienna hair popped back into her seat at the receptionist's desk from a narrow door directly behind it. "May I help you?"

"Yes, I've come to pick up Caleb Hunter. I guess he's still in with Mr. Miner?"

"He is not," said the woman. "Mr. Hunter missed his appointment."

"Missed—but I saw him come in that door," Meg said, pointing.

"He went across the street for a cup of coffee and never came back," explained the receptionist, holding out a sheet of paper. "I called the number he provided, but I didn't get an answer."

Meg glanced at the extended paper. There wouldn't have been an answer at the number Caleb had written down. It was hers, and if he'd actually headed home, he would have been on foot and wouldn't be there yet. Besides, he didn't have a key.

Spinning on her heel, Meg looked toward the coffee shop, unable to see inside through the glare on the window glass. With a hasty thank you, Meg left the office and crossed the street. Inside the shop, Meg gave the empty café a quick once-over before addressing the teenager behind the counter. "Did you have a customer earlier, a dark haired man about six-foot-three wearing a tan coat?" she asked him.

The young man glanced up from a folded newspaper on the counter. "Do you expect me to remember every customer who comes in here?"

Meg indicated the tables with a wave of her hand. "Doesn't look all that busy. You could at least try to be helpful." A single cup at an empty table caught her eye. "Maybe he'd been sitting there?" she suggested.

Noting the direction of her study, the young man straightened from his perusal of the want ads. "Oh, that guy. Yeah, he might be the one you're looking for. I left that there because I thought he might be coming back."

Meg walked over to peer into the lidless cup. An oily slick filmed the top of the dark liquid, apparently quite cold. No one would be hastening back for that particular beverage. "Did you see which way the man went when he left?"

The teen shrugged.

Heading back out into the chilly sunlight, Meg paused on the sidewalk to view the street in both directions. Where would Caleb have gone? And why?

"Oh, God," she whispered. Might he have suffered an aggravation of whatever caused his memory loss? Walked out of the coffee shop recalling nothing at all, not even her? Or had he remembered everything? She realized the second scenario might be the most frightening to him. How would he react when he recalled the moments leading up to the fight for his life? The names and faces of the men who had been with him?

Meg slid into the driver's seat of her car, clutched the ridged plastic of the wheel, and leaned her forehead against her knuckles. The photographic images she had seen in the police station circled in a frantic dance inside her head. Meg finally turned the key in the ignition and backed the car out of the parking space. As she drove, she stared down side streets and into the faces of people she passed, hoping to spot Caleb among them. Repeatedly, she backtracked to the area near Craig Miner's office, checking the broad window of the coffee shop and the sidewalks outside. She called the investigator's number to ask the receptionist if he'd returned. She called home, listening to the phone ring and ring, hanging up when voice mail came on. No point in a message. Caleb wouldn't have any idea how to retrieve it. Besides, he had no way of getting in.

Finally, she headed back to her house. If Caleb had any concept at all of where he was, he would make his way back to her house on his own. She didn't want to consider what steps might be necessary if she didn't find him there.

Meg cut the engine in the driveway and clutched the keys in her fist as she studied the front of her house. One of the lower panes of glass on the front door had been broken. Her heart skipped a beat, then steadied as she remembered the damage couldn't have been caused by Matt. Caleb must have broken the pane to enter the house.

With a mingling of relief and trepidation, Meg exited the car and walked to the front door. A few shards of glass sparkled on the doorstep.

The rest, she knew, would be lying on the hardwood floor inside. Turning the unlocked knob, Meg pushed the door open and stepped over the threshold.

Tossing her keys on the table beside the door, she called Caleb's name. He appeared from the kitchen as she removed her coat.

"I'll fix that if you show me how," he said in subdued tones.

Meg hung her coat and scarf on the coatrack, clinging a moment to the fabric in her hands. "How long have you been back?" she asked, without turning.

"About a half an hour."

"You walked?"

He didn't answer. She glanced at him over her shoulder and saw him nod.

"What happened with the private investigator?"

"I didn't see him."

"I know that," Meg said with forbearance. "Why not?"

She would listen to all he had to say before she gave him her news. She needed more time to get her head around what she had learned at the police department. Though bewildered and sad, she wasn't afraid. Once she said the words aloud, asked the questions she needed to ask, showed Caleb the photograph she had pilfered from Agent Phillips' collection, she would be afraid. But by then, there would be no turning back.

Caleb came to her and wrapped his arms around her back. He pulled her up against his chest. She raised her arms to encircle his waist, scrubbing her cheek back and forth across the soft fabric of his shirt. His heart beat beneath her ear, steady and strong and seemingly unaffected by the currents of strangeness swirling between them.

"You're like ice," she whispered.

"It was a long walk," he said above her head.

"Why didn't you wait for me?"

"I couldn't." She felt his lips against her hair, the tightening of the muscles of his arms before he released her. "Come into the kitchen."

She followed him down the dim hallway with an odd lack of physical sensation. She supposed it could be hysteria.

In the open doorway, she paused, her gaze caught by the sight of Matt's old sweatshirt jacket hanging on the hook. She reached out and touched it, fingering a frayed hole in the elbow. "Matt's dead," she said, unable to hold back. "He's been dead for a few weeks."

The words sounded flat to her ears. If Caleb experienced any surprise at the news, he gave no indication. She couldn't even be certain he'd heard her.

"Sit down," he directed, pointing to a chair he'd pulled from the table.

She perched on the edge of the seat as Caleb eased himself into the chair opposite. His eyes held hers with an expression of haunted determination.

"Today...today I had my photograph taken in a booth in the coffee shop across from the investigator's office." He pulled three strips of photographs from beneath the napkin holder. He slid them across the table to her.

"I thought it might be a good idea to give them to the investigator. When I saw the photos my first thought was, why didn't she tell me? But then I realized, you couldn't. You couldn't tell me anything. There was no way you could know what I saw when I looked out of my eyes."

Meg separated the three strips, side by side, her fingers splayed along the edges. The first set was useless, his face hidden from view, and the second was almost comical, his expression purposeful as he tried to focus on the task of having his picture taken in a manner no doubt foreign to him. In the third set, however, his dismay, even horror, reared evident as he stared at the lens.

"That's me," he stated quietly. "Isn't it? I mean, it has to be...right?"

Meg nodded, wondering what he had thought he looked like, what he had seen in the mirror every morning, what he had seen reflected in her eyes. Swallowing, she reached into her pants pocket for the crumpled photograph she had hidden in her scarf at the police station and placed the photo on the table with the others. She spun all of them around so they faced Caleb.

He grimaced, bending closer to stare down at the one she had taken from Agent Phillips. He rubbed his forefinger across the likeness of himself, then pointed to the other man in the FBI photo. "Who is that?" he asked in a harsh voice, as if he found the inquiry difficult to articulate.

Meg bit her lip. He didn't remember. What would happen when he did? "That's Matt," she whispered.

* * * *

She told him to keep the money designated for the private investigator and gave him more. She packed the clothes she'd bought him in a bag, as well as all of Matt's that she'd never thrown away. He might need them.

Agent Phillips had supplied her with a minimum of information about the other man in the photograph with Matt when he walked her to the door of the police station. His name was, indeed, Caleb Hunter, but the name was an alias. He couldn't tell her Caleb's true identity, as the whole incident remained under investigation. But she understood Caleb and Matt had been closely acquainted for more than a year.

"Did this man kill Matt?" she'd asked.

But Agent Phillips couldn't, or wouldn't, tell her. So after she had left him, she'd spent hours searching for a man who might have killed her husband, and when she found him returned to her home, she had given that same man her money—only realizing later how incriminating that might look—and a kiss goodbye. In that contact, her mouth on his own, with the breath of his lungs filling hers, she had relived again the vision of his fight for his life, one man against two others. If Caleb had taken Matt's life in defense of his own, then so be it. But he needed his past returned to him, no matter what it held.

"I have to know who I am, Meg. What I am," Caleb said to her at the door. "I can't do it here with you. I can't ask questions of the authorities. I can't do it except on my own. I don't know why, but I know that's true."

Meg nodded at him, touching his face one last time. He turned his face against her palm, pressing his lips to the pulse in her wrist.

"Get as far away from here as you can, Caleb. They're looking for you now."

He held her for a long time while she cried in his arms, and then he was gone. She didn't expect to ever see him again.

Chapter 22

Meg reached up to pull the chain on the kitchen light fixture, hesitating with her hand in the air, frowning at the calendar on the wall. She'd forgotten to flip to the new month. Removing the clip, she re-affixed the new page to reveal a snowy December scene. Caleb had been gone for a little over three weeks without any word. Shortly after his departure, Agent Phillips and the one from Interpol, Stefan Andre, had questioned her again, after which they, too, had exited her life. She returned to the routine of her days, altered now by Caleb's absence. It sometimes felt emptier than when Matt had gone away.

She had arranged another funeral, quiet and unpublicized, to inter Matthew Donovan's remains, attending the service with Matt's aged aunt and her daughter, the only relatives remaining of his small family. They hadn't asked questions, no doubt having received all the information needed from other sources, and Meg had been grateful for their silence and for their presence at the brief memorial for her husband. This time, she hadn't cried.

Frowning at the calendar, Meg flipped it back to November, then back to October, touching with the tip of her finger the small check mark she made habitually every month. She thought for a moment, hard, scanning the days of November for a similar mark and not finding one.

She'd missed her period.

Closing her eyes, Meg swore softly under her breath, letting the calendar pages flutter from her fingers. She clutched her abdomen, remembering with a heated flush the night with Caleb when they hadn't used protection. She turned on her heel and walked into the living room. Sitting on the couch, she shoved her face in her hands.

"Don't panic," she whispered against the heels of her palms. "Don't panic."

She lifted her head, staring across the room at the shelf of books she'd illustrated. She rose and crossed the rug to take one down, letting it fall open in her hands. Caleb had been more astute than most, recognizing the similarities in all the illustrations. Anne. Sweet Anne.

A bubble of grief and fear and sadness welled up in her throat, choking off air. Tears slid down her cheeks. With the flat of her fingers, Meg stroked the paper, the golden hair of the child depicted in the story. This one, more than any other, resembled her daughter.

"Will you forgive me if I have another?" she asked the silent, smiling picture. Closing the book, she returned the volume to the shelf, went back to turn off the kitchen light, and climbed the stairs to bed.

In her loneliness, she dreamed of Caleb. Dreamed of his long, heated body, his mouth on her, the touch of his hands, the searing, slow intensity with which he made love. When she woke, flushed, damp with sweat, and acutely aroused, she found a weight in the bed beside her.

A hand closed gently across her mouth before she could cry out.

"Meg."

Struggling out from under his fingers, Meg threw her arms around him, whispering his name over and over against his ear. *Caleb.* Had he learned this was not his name? It didn't matter. She would always think of him that way.

"Oh, Caleb, I missed you." She kissed his face, his mouth, his eyes.

"I missed you, too. And didn't I say I didn't want to do that?"

He sounded different, no doubt altered by the journey he had taken in search of himself. She wondered if he had come any closer to finding out his identity, but she hesitated to ask him, rising up onto her knees instead to unzip the suede jacket she'd bought him, still smelling like the cold night. She pushed it off his shoulders, yanked the sleeves from his arms. He lay with his dark head on her pillow, eyes following her movements as she removed his shoes, his pants.

"You're freezing cold. Get under the blankets."

Silently, he obeyed. She crawled under the covers beside him, trying to warm his limbs. "Oh, Caleb," she said again.

"Shh."

Several times, she opened her mouth to ask him what news he had and kept silent, fearful of the answer. She stroked his chest, slipping her hand beneath his shirt to trail her fingers through the silky hair running up from his flat belly.

"You've lost weight. Have you not been eating? Do you want me to make you something?"

"No," he said, pushing her hand down lower on his body. As she stroked him through the soft material of his boxers, his eyes closed and a small sigh slipped past his lips. His penis grew hard under her attention, and the sounds he made grew deeper.

"Take your clothes off, Meg, will you? I don't have the strength."

"Are you all right?"

"I'm just tired. I feel like the life has been sapped out of me. You'll give it back to me, though. I know you will."

Stripping out of her long-sleeved shirt and flannel pants, Meg pressed her naked body against him. He turned toward her, the entire length of his body thrumming as if with electricity, the charge of it singing in her blood. He touched her between the legs. "Were you dreaming about me?"

"Yes," she said.

"Good."

Pulling her on top of him, he parted her legs with his knees. Meg slid his boxers off, reaching with her other hand to the drawer of the nightstand. He grabbed her wrist, slipping two fingers of his other hand inside of her. She gasped at the remembered sensation, a shudder coursing over her skin.

"Leave the box in the drawer, Meg," he said.

"I shouldn't," she breathed.

"Does it matter now?" he asked. "You're pregnant."

"I—what?"

"You're carrying his child when you wouldn't carry mine."

Meg froze. "What?" she asked again, the word barely escaping her throat. All the while his fingers continued their exploration, coldly, as if what he did to her didn't matter to him. The hand gripping her wrist held on with painful tightness.

"You fucked him here in our bed, Meg. Hid him from Stauffer and those other two. Gave him money and wished him well, even when you thought he'd killed me."

Twisting furiously, Meg pulled free, leaping from the bed. She grabbed her clothes and put them on, standing at the foot of the mattress. He lay on his back, the curve of his mouth sinister.

"Caleb," she said.

"Stop calling me that. That's not my name."

She took a step away. "It's the only name I've known for you. Who is it you think you are? Did you find out?"

The smile grew broader, stretching into a grin, and not a grin she remembered seeing on Caleb's face. Leaping across the room, she turned on the light. The darkness frightened her. Caleb frightened her.

"It's me, sweetheart," Caleb said from the bed, drawing out the last part of the last word with an upward turn of the *a* and *r*. He lifted himself up on his elbows. "Your husband."

Oh, Jesus. Meg stumbled backward against the computer stool and sat down.

He'd lost his mind. He hadn't found anything—he'd lost it all. Or perhaps he'd discovered entirely too much, and guilt about killing Matt had unhinged him. And what? Made Caleb think he was Matt?

"I don't think I'm Matt," Caleb announced from the bed, reading her thoughts as she had once suspected he could. "I am Matt."

Her abdomen clenched as if she'd been punched. "No. You're not." In this state, he could be dangerous. She needed to get out of this room and to the phone.

"Won't work."

"What won't work?" she demanded, voice rising.

"The phone. I yanked the line outside."

"Caleb, please."

"Don't call me that!"

He tore out of the bed so quickly she almost didn't see him move. He stood before her now in nothing but his shirt and socks, his erection still raging. Every inch of him Caleb's body, but the stance not his at all.

"I was on my way back to you, did you know that? Had a job up this way, and I knew you'd be overjoyed to find out I hadn't died, hadn't drowned in the cold, black sea, the end you always feared for me." He nearly spat in his sarcasm. "Me and Caleb, we go back a-ways. Told that bastard everything about my life, every detail."

The history between them, the conversations about her life with Matt, could explain Caleb's knowledge of intimate details of Matt's actions, could have caused him to act them out subconsciously. His behavior even now could be explained by—

"No," said Caleb, with fierce enunciation, "that doesn't explain anything."

Oh, dear God, she prayed. Their thoughts had often entered into each other's minds, hers and Caleb's, but not like this.

"How sweet," Caleb drawled, coming to stand in front of her. He dropped his shorts to the floor and grabbed the back of her neck, yanking her forward, mashing her turned cheek against his stiff penis. "You know what I want."

She punched him hard in the thigh and shoved him backward, catching him in the testicle with the edge of her hand. He bent forward with a groan. As she scrambled to her feet, he straightened.

"Get out of my house," she said, teeth clenched.

He arched a single eyebrow at her in a responsive gesture she recognized. Her hand came up to her mouth, holding back a scream. "It can't be you," she whispered through her fingers.

Reaching down, Caleb pulled up his shorts and stretched an arm back to retrieve his pants. Stepping into them, he hoisted them to his waist. "It can," he said, walking around the bed, "and it is. You're so willing to believe all that crap about your dreams and your thoughts, why not this?"

Meg shook her head. Caleb extended his hand to the lamp, pulling off the shade. "Come here."

"I don't think so," Meg answered, her gaze sliding to the door.

"You're not leaving, Meg. I said come here."

She lunged in the direction of the door, fingers arching for the knob, her blood pumping. Fire tore across the back of her skull as he grabbed a fistful of hair and stopped her short. Locks knotted through his fingers, he dragged her back to the bed.

"Look at me," he growled.

He lifted the lamp in his hand, the heat of the bare bulb grazing the skin of her cheek. Abruptly he moved the lamp away, to his own face. Meg raised her eyes. "No!"

In that instant, unguarded, not knowing what to expect with the light bright and white against his skin, she had seen Matt, possessing the body she'd come to care so much about, brown eyes looking more like the color of the earth than of the sea. But she had seen more than Matt had thought to show her. Caleb remained behind those eyes, too.

"Not for long," Matt said. "He's a dying soul."

"I don't understand," Meg whispered.

"There's nothing to understand," said Matt conversationally, maintaining his killer grip on her scalp. "He pretended to be my friend. You led him to me."

"I—what?"

"I knew you had. Made me furious, that did. I'd been duped, took him in, let him share the riches, so to speak, and then I found out it was all a lie. Subterfuge," he said, with exaggerated slowness. "He was an agent for Interpol. Gary and I, we decided to take care of that out on the ocean.

Figured it was easy after what we did to Jimmy and Donald, but it wasn't. Bastard knew something was coming and fought like the fucking devil. Gary got dumped in the sea. Don't think he made it. Then your buddy Caleb, he killed me."

Meg lowered her lashes, a long shudder snaking through skin tissue and muscle.

"But I didn't die right away. There was this moment, this one infinitesimal moment of...of gleaming darkness, it was, when I saw my chance and took it. Struck a deal with the devil. But Caleb sensed something had happened, and even though he didn't know what it was, the fucker ran the boat aground before we got here. *My* boat."

She recalled the piece of Matt's boat Dan had found washed up on the beach. So like Matt in his arrogance not to have changed the name. How had Caleb gotten to this particular stretch of beach when there had been no sign of wreckage?

"He was sick and beat up rather badly," Matt went on, voluble in his desire to torment. "And afraid. I could read his fear. Not of me, never of me, that whole time. Afraid of what I'd do to you when I got here. Christ, he didn't even know you. What the fuck should he care?"

Oh, Caleb.

"Oh, Caleb," he mimicked, jerking her head back so she faced him again.

"Matt, please."

"Hey," he said, almost conversationally, "did you ever figure out my little message on the table?"

She shook her head, wincing at the tug of her hair between his fingers.

"'I had to leave you'" he quoted. "And I did have to leave you. You knew me better than anyone. I couldn't stand the daily reminders that I wasn't the man you married. I hated you for that. I never liked the man you married. I liked the man I became. The man I was before Caleb killed me. That *is* his name, you know. Caleb, but not Hunter. Caleb Russell. Want to know how I know that?"

"No!"

"Too bad. I'm telling you whether you want to hear or not. It's because I've been holding onto his memories for him, took them away and kept them from him. Still, he managed to fight me until I made him see me. Really see me. See me inside of him. Shock did it. Forced him to let go after sharing this body of his for, what, six weeks? Funny, how he kept picking up on memories of mine during that time. So I took advantage of that. Did you like the initials on the mirror? I made him write those. And the stupid thing you have with the towel on the stove. I mean, shit, Meg, are you still so anal? I thought the perfect touch were those freaking paper flowers. Drove you crazy, didn't it? I watched him fuck you, too. I wasn't liking that much at all."

Reaching up behind her head, Meg dug her fingers into his. "Matt, let me go."

"No," he stated simply and swung her with unnatural strength onto the bed, pinning her with his arms and legs. "My turn, now," he whispered.

Meg bucked and bit, pushed and scratched, aware Caleb's body received the damage and feeling the pain like her own. Matt laughed, pressing his mouth to her throat and to her breasts through her shirt, then finally lifted his head to look her in the eye. "After I'm done here," he whispered, "we'll talk about how you're going to die, too."

Bringing her head forward with all her strength, Meg crashed her skull against Matt's cheekbone, missing the more disabling strike against his nose. Nevertheless, he reeled back, momentarily releasing her. Meg rolled away, landing on the floor with a force that nearly knocked the breath from her lungs. She leapt up as Matt rose to stand on the sagging mattress. His eyes met hers. Caleb's tea-brown eyes, the inner struggle contorting his face.

"Run, Meg," came the strangled command.

Meg raced down the back stairs and into the kitchen, spinning on her bare heel in search of her cell phone and keys. Neither sat where she'd left them earlier. No time to keep looking. She had to get out of the house.

Hands slick with fear, she fumbled twice with the lock on the door before releasing the catch. Yanking the door open, she fled into the frigid night, Matt's bellowing rage echoing through the house as she pounded to the far end of the porch. Vaulting over the railing, she landed in a heap in the sand beyond. A sob tore from her throat. Pushing to her feet, she ran toward the road.

At the sound of boots on shingles, she glanced back, almost losing her footing. Matt hadn't bothered with the stairs. Caleb's body stood silhouetted against the open bedroom window as his head jerked in search of her. Meg veered further out into the sand. Matt launched himself from the roof, landing with a grunting roll a yard or two in front of her and leaping to his feet.

Heart pounding, Meg reversed and raced across the garden, throwing first the gazing ball and then kicking the fire pit into Matt's path in her wake. Stumbling down the rickety steps to the desolate beach, she knew no possibility of help existed there. She could only hope to outrun him, make it to the jetty and hide. Though loud and clumsy in his fury, Matt was only seconds behind her.

Meg hammered through cold sand in her bare feet, blood singing in her ears, the blooming cloud of her breath freezing as it curled into her nostrils, the sound of her pulse and the surf drowning out the noise of Matt's pursuit. She didn't dare look back for fear of losing her footing again. No sooner had the thought entered her mind and her ankle turned, snapped. She flew to the sand a dozen feet in front of the purling surf. He pounced on her before she could regain her breath.

"Matt! No!"

Dragging her by the arm and the back of her pants, he bumped her over the uneven terrain to the water's edge, her broken ankle jarring across the sand. Still, she fought him, twisting in his grip.

"Matt, please!"

"You were always afraid of the sea, weren't you, Meg?" he taunted, pulling her into the water. The surf broke over her, saltwater running into her nose, her mouth. She choked and gasped for air. He pushed her back down under the surging tide and lifted her up again.

"Afraid of drowning. Afraid of me drowning. You made your fear my own. And guess what? That's how I died. Sinking into the blackness with Caleb in my boat, watching."

Meg tossed the sodden hair from her eyes. A sickle moon shone in the sky above Matt's head. "I saw a photo of your body, Matt," she cried. "You didn't drown! Your body washed up on shore with no water in your lungs! If you had waited before you embraced the darkness, you might have lived."

"You lie," he snarled.

"I'm not lying!" she said as he began to push her under again. "I'm not lying. Look in my eyes, Matt. Look! You know I'm telling the truth."

He howled with the inner rage she knew had always been his, shoving both her shoulders under the dark tide, the sound of the water in her ears a deep, singing, deadening silence despite its movement. She struggled against his weight, against the force of the water, against the urge to open her mouth and let the ocean in, to let it take her away from the nightmare of knowing what Matt had done and fear that Caleb would soon be no more. With a final effort before her lungs burst, she dug her hands down in an effort to push her body upward and found beneath her fingers the shape of something long and solid slowly being released from its bed in the sand by the pull of the receding tide.

Caleb, she pleaded as she pulled the pipe from the sucking sand, *forgive me.*

Chapter 23

"Oh, God," Meg sobbed. With every ounce of her strength, she pulled Caleb's lifeless body from the surf, her good foot pressed deep into the sand. Lifting his head into her lap, she opened her fingers across his bloody scalp. By her broken ankle, the rusted pipe lay, matted with strands of Caleb's soft, dark hair. She pressed her face to his, searching for evidence of breath, then lay the fingers of her other hand against his neck for the remembered beat of his strong and steady pulse.

Nothing.

"Caleb, no. No, no, no."

Arching her neck, she screamed at the sky.

With a gasp, she brought her head back down beside his. "Caleb, don't be dead," she whispered. "I love you. I love you."

Twisting at the waist, she started shouting for help. A futile exercise. No one would hear her. She'd stayed in this house despite the pain associated with it because of the isolation.

"Oh, God," she said again as she shifted her body to lower Caleb's head to the sand. The skin of his throat, his face, was like ice in her hands. Dragging her leg with its shattered ankle to position it by the other, she forced herself to roll over onto her knees. Biting down at the grinding of bone, she tasted blood on her chilled lip.

Somewhere in her house was her cell phone. If she crawled across the beach and up the stairs, she could call for help, could get someone to save Caleb. Because he wasn't dead. She refused to believe he was dead. But she had no illusions as to how long it would take her to cross the sand, how she might lose him in that time.

Reaching for Caleb's hand, she drew his fingers into her own, barely able to feel them as she began to succumb, in her soaked nightclothes, to the frigid temperatures. Could she perform CPR? Did she even remember how? Would it matter when she'd bashed his head in so ruthlessly?

"Caleb, Caleb, forgive me." On her knees still, she tried to recall what she could of resuscitation. Leaning over him, she crossed her hands against his chest. Something hard protruded from his shirt pocket and she shoved it away. A second later, realization of the object's identity hit her and she wrestled a cell phone from the tangled fabric.

Her cell phone.

Her smashed cell phone.

Throwing the useless instrument down in the sand, she began to pound on Caleb's chest with her fists clamped together. With every strike, his body jerked like a puppet's. "Please, Caleb. Please. Don't leave me."

"Meg."

Gasping, she stared at Caleb's face, finding his mouth still slack, his eyes nearly closed, unmoving.

"Meg," said the voice again. A hand grabbed her arm, pulling her back onto her broken extremity. She cried out.

"Meg," said the voice a third time, "what the hell?"

"Dan!"

Jerking around, she stared up at his face, the circles beneath his eyes dark and heavy. He pushed past her and stretched out his hand, checking the pulse in Caleb's neck.

"Save him, Dan. Don't let him die."

"What the fuck happened?"

"I—" How much could she tell him? "I hit him with that pipe. He isn't dead, is he? Please don't tell me I killed him."

And yet that had been her intent, to drive Matt from Caleb's body. Not so much to save herself as to free Caleb before Matt's dark soul destroyed his.

Dan pulled his cell phone out and began speaking into it, giving her address to the 911 operator. "Send an ambulance. Now. Don't know if this guy is going to make it, but I'm getting a thready pulse. He's out on the beach behind the house. Tell them to freaking hurry."

Meg crawled forward, pressing her lips to Caleb's cold forehead. The blood had stopped flowing, though the sand behind his head looked black in the moonlight from seepage. "Stay with me, Caleb. Just you, Caleb. Just you. I love you."

She raised her eyes to find Dan shrugging out of his coat. He draped it over Caleb's chest. "Sorry. He needs it more than you do."

Meg nodded. She shoved her hand into Caleb's splayed fingers and squeezed, hard.

"What happened here, Meg?"

Meg bit her lip, bowing her head. Salt moisture from her eyes mingled with the salt and sand from the ocean on her face. "I... Dan, I don't know if you'll believe me. If you can believe me. Matt... Matt was trying to kill me."

"Matt? You mean Caleb."

"No," said Meg. "I mean Matt."

She raised her gaze to Dan's, staring at him through her wet, tangled hair. His eyes widened.

"Don't. Don't tell me. Not here on this beach. Wait until we're away. Better still, wait until the light of day."

In the distance, the sirens of an ambulance pierced the rising wind. Meg huddled over Caleb's body to protect him from the blowing sand and the dropping temperature. She observed no breath, no pulse, but Dan's training for this type of emergency made him better equipped. He would know. He would *know*.

"Dan."

"What?"

"Is he going to die?"

Dan didn't answer. Meg cupped Caleb's immobile jaw, the stubble of beard rough on her fingers. She kissed his mouth, hoping somewhere deep in his subconscious he would be aware of the caress and it would give him the strength to hold on. Recalling Matt's eyes in Caleb's face, though, she drew away and turned to Dan, finding him watching her with a hollow expression in his pale blue gaze.

Rising suddenly, he flipped on the flashlight in his phone and began to wave it. Meg heard voices on the rise by her house. Less than a minute later a trio of men in uniform arrived, pulling her from Caleb's side. They worked with a minimal amount of discussion, preparing Caleb's body for transport on a stretcher. Meg sat shivering in the sand, wondering whose eyes would be looking back at her when Caleb finally awakened.

Wondering if he ever would.

* * * *

Meg lay perfectly still. Hospital personnel had rushed Caleb from the emergency room to an operating room long before anyone had the chance to look at her ankle. He was alive. For now only, perhaps, but a tiny thrill of hope had surfaced at the realization and continued to run along the surface of her skin like cool water.

The curtain of the cubicle parted. She expected it would be the orderly coming to take her to X-ray. Instead, she found Dan's tired eyes gazing back at hers.

"I guess I'll have to tell them when they take me down to X-ray that I might be pregnant," she said.

"You're what?" He came inside in a hurry, standing at the foot of the bed. He appeared nervous and clumsy and oddly endearing for a man she had never cared for.

"Pregnant. Don't tell Caleb, though. I want to."

Dan stepped to the side and sat abruptly in a white plastic chair. He folded his hands between his knees, staring at her.

"I know," she said. "I'm not making much sense. But he's going to be all right. Isn't he?"

The sensation of coursing water dissipated a fraction, hope dampened by reality. The pain in her ankle flared.

"Meg...."

"Why were you at my house tonight, Dan? Don't get me wrong. I'll be forever grateful for it. I'm just wondering."

He didn't reply straightaway, taking the time to flick sand from his trousers onto the floor. He turned to look out through the parted curtain, as if to make certain no one was listening. His shoulders moved, tensing beneath his jacket, and then slumped as he faced her again.

"Meg, I've been watching your house for a while. Don't," he said, forestalling speech from her, although she had no intention of interrupting him. "Even though we all believed Matt's ship had gone down, I'd always felt there was some unfinished business. He'd gotten involved with some very nasty people, and I thought some of his associates might one day come to the house, thinking cash or drugs or stolen goods might be hidden there. He was into it all. Eventually, I just watched your house to be sure you were all right." He shrugged. "And one night—I tried to tell you about it outside the drugstore—I saw something on the beach and, later, in your attic through the window. I was in the car with Phillips and Andre that time. They didn't see a thing. I'd thought maybe I'd gone a little mad, you know?"

Meg said nothing. She could relate. As to Matt's crimes, well, someday, she might learn more, but right now, it didn't matter.

"What I saw was...was like a negative of a photograph, if you can visualize a living, animated negative of a photograph. A dark thing that made my soul shrivel. I don't know if it was a ghost or what the hell it was. But it had something to do with your boyfriend. Somehow I knew that much."

Shifting her leg on the stiff, narrow mattress, Meg grimaced. "It wasn't Caleb. Not Caleb. It was Matt."

A muscle in Dan's jaw twitched.

"Caleb knew Matt, you see," Meg continued, leaning forward. "He was an agent for Interpol investigating Matt and infiltrated his operations, working with him undercover."

"How do you know that?"

"That he was an agent for Interpol? Matt told me. Tonight."

Dan's tongue slipped out to moisten his lips. He rubbed a hand over his jaw. "Go on."

"Matt tried to kill Caleb on Matt's boat, and they struggled. Matt... Matt possessed Caleb's body before he...well, before his body died."

"Meg, that's nuts."

"Is it? Think about what you saw."

He remained silent a long time. A wheeled cart squeaked past. Someone nearby cried out in pain. The nurses chattered on as if the world was normal. "How is that possible?"

Meg shook her head. "I don't know. But when Caleb came to me tonight, Matt had control of him. That's why, oh God, that's why I hit him. He was trying to kill me."

Meg brought her hands up to her face. Dan rose from the chair, the metal legs sliding on the floor. She felt his fingers on her wrists, pulling them down, and resisted.

"Look at me," he said. "Just look at me."

He released her and she dropped her hands. His chest lifted and fell several times before he spoke. "Meg, if what you're saying is true, then who the hell is going to be waking up from that operating table?"

Fighting nausea, Meg let out a slow breath. She reached to touch the knuckles of his fist curled on the edge of the mattress. "Caleb. Please God," she prayed, "it has to be Caleb."

Chapter 24

Meg fitted the pair of crutches beneath her arms, curling her fingers around the crosspieces. She hadn't quite gotten used to walking encumbered by extensions to her limbs in the week she'd been on them.

"All set?" asked the doctor, arching his eyebrows behind the rim of his glasses.

"Yes, Dr. Redecker. Thank you for your help with these," she added, indicating the crutches by swinging the right one away from her body several inches.

"Lucky it was your left foot. At least you can still drive. Sometime today or tomorrow, I want you to get over to the drugstore and get this prescription filled. Prenatal vitamins are extremely important."

Meg thanked him again and left the office with the prescription shoved into her purse. She hobbled down the short flight of stairs and across the parking lot to her car. Easing behind the steering wheel, she set the crutches in the passenger seat and sat for a moment, staring down the street to the place where the sailors' cross stood stark against the sky.

Sleeping pills might have helped her with the horrifying nightmares, but pregnant women couldn't take sleeping pills.

Pregnant. Despite all her years of dread and dismissal, even the uncertainty of her future, she smiled and put the car in reverse. Backing from the parking space, she headed out of town in the direction of the hospital, the hospital where, one day, God willing, she would give birth to her child.

The nurses on the third floor hurried to help her, but she waved them away. Maybe she had begun to get the hang of the crutches, after all, because she managed to make her way in bumping slowness along the hallway to Room 316 in ICU without mishap. Outside the glass wall of the room, she stood gazing in at Caleb's prone form on the bed. The bronze of his skin had faded, leaving him as pale as the sheets. His lashes lay in shadow against the bluish tint of the flesh beneath his eyes. His long, dark hair tangled over his neck from under the bandages wrapped around his damaged, healing skull. For several minutes, she watched him, hesitant to enter. Today would be different than all the other days since he'd come out of the operating room still clinging to life. Today would be harder. Today would affect the rest of her life.

Because today Caleb had opened his eyes and spoken.

As she made her decision to enter, a familiar voice stopped her. She pivoted on the heel of her cast. "Dan," she greeted him without animosity. "What are you doing here?"

"I come every now and then," he said, pausing beside her to stare in at Caleb as she had done. "I sit with him. I wait. I want to know who's going to look out of those eyes, too."

Meg sighed. "He spoke to one of the nurses today."

"I know."

"I'm afraid to go in there."

"I know."

"They'll only let one of us in at a time."

"It should be you," said Dan. "I've got my eye on one of those pretty nurses anyway. It might be time for a chat."

"But—"

"You see anything you don't like in there, you yell."

Nodding, Meg slid the door open and stepped inside. She pushed the door closed, shutting out Dan's greeting to the red-haired nurse. Rhythmically beeping machines kept track of Caleb's vital signs without overriding the sound of his breathing. She listened hard to the in and out of each breath, searching for a hitch, an indication of labor, of struggle, but his respiration remained steady. After setting her purse on a chair, she maneuvered her way to the side of the bed.

"Caleb." *Please, please, please be Caleb.*

He didn't stir. She leaned her crutches against the wall.

"Caleb."

With painful slowness, his lids lifted, his unfocused gaze settling somewhere in the middle of the room until she spoke again. She held her breath. His eyes shifted toward her. Not eyes the deep brown of peat. Tea-brown eyes, clear and lucid.

"Oh, Caleb," she breathed. Moisture blurred her vision and rolled down her cheeks.

"Meg," he croaked.

And he knew who she was. She had feared she'd wounded him more grievously than Matt had done, and his brain would be damaged beyond repair. Witnessing his struggle to speak, Meg grabbed a swab from the bedside table and moistened his mouth and lips as she wept above his head.

"Stop," he whispered, turning his face away from her ministrations. "Come...here."

Careful not to tangle in his many wires and intravenous tubes, Meg climbed right up in the bed with him, hoisting her casted foot onto the tangled sheets with both hands.

Wrapping his arm around her, he gave her a weak squeeze. "What... what happened to your...foot?"

"I broke my ankle. It doesn't matter. What matters is that you're here."

"Here," he echoed and appeared to be drifting off as she lay against him, his heartbeat strong beneath her ear. After a moment, he rallied. "Where is...here?"

"County Hospital. Room 316."

"I see...I'm in a hospital. Why?"

Meg squeezed her eyes shut, fighting back more tears. She and Dan had reached an agreement to tell Caleb the same story they'd told Dan's department, that after an argument with her, Caleb had tripped and fallen, smashing his head on a rock on the beach. But she couldn't bring herself to lie. Not when she'd so nearly lost him.

"Caleb."

"Did I hurt you?"

Meg stiffened, her breath catching in her lungs. "What?"

"I remember...trying to. I remember so many strange things."

"Hush, Caleb. Don't talk now. Rest."

"My head hurts."

"I know. Just be still for a while."

He complied, his body slumping in her embrace. After several minutes, though, he spoke again. "I remember who I am."

She bit her lip, overwhelmed with a sudden fear that he would say her husband's name.

"I am...Caleb, after all. I got that right."

Nodding against him, she waited for him to catch his breath and continue.

"I'm...I'm an agent for Interpol. Most recently...operating out of the Bahamas...where I was investigating your husband...."

Meg shut her eyes, her entire body going cold. She wanted him to stop, to stop speaking, stop remembering, yet she needed to hear it all.

"I...I killed him, Meg."

No. You didn't. I did.

"He attacked me. Him...and Gary. They worked together."

She knew this from Matt. She kept silent. Caleb tugged several strands of her hair between his pointer and thumb. She turned her face against the warmth seeping through his hospital gown. His chest rose and fell beneath her cheek.

"He knew someone had given him up. That he was being watched." He took a moment, whether in recollection or for strength, she couldn't tell. "He blamed you, Meg. Got it fixated in his mind that you'd gone to the authorities with information here in the States and that he was being hunted because of that."

"When I thought all this time he was dead? Besides, I didn't know anything for certain. I never turned on him. Well, not until I thought he'd come back."

"I'm sorry, Meg, but I think he'd lost his mind at that point. He was obviously unstable when I met him. Not that it matters anymore...but he planned to kill you. Talked about it as calmly as you might talk about plans for dinner."

Meg stared at a posted notice on the wall, visualizing Caleb's face against the blue paper but with Matt's eyes. She suppressed a shiver. "And you stepped in."

"At first, I tried to hammer home the risk...of coming back here. He didn't care. And then...and then, I blew my cover."

He tensed against her. "Shh," said Meg. "Let it go. You can't think about any of that right now."

He didn't argue, and after a moment he relaxed, his spine sinking into the curve of the mattress. Outside the glass, Dan had stepped close, hands in his pockets. Meg met his eyes across the room. He nodded in acknowledgment of her position splayed across Caleb's rib cage. Clearly, it hadn't been Matt who'd returned to the world.

"What's Stauffer doing here?"

Meg pushed up on the mattress, studying Caleb's face. His gaze shifted from Dan's to hers. No anger. Only curiosity and a touch of confusion.

"He helped save you," she said. "I think maybe he just wants to make sure you're all right."

"Huh. Maybe you'll have to explain that all to me later."

In the corridor, Dan turned on his heel and walked away. Meg settled back down onto Caleb's chest.

"Caleb, I—"

"I have no wife, Meg…no children. I used to have a dog…a long time ago. No encumbrances. Nothing calling me back. My life is my own."

"And I'm still in it," Meg said quietly.

"Always, I hope. When I left you…I missed you so much. I just wandered. Up and down the coast, asking questions, finding out nothing. I wanted so badly to come back to you. I think it weakened me, somehow. I don't mean that the way it sounds. But it was then that I…that I started to…lose my grip on…everything. I swear I remember—"

"No." Struggling up again, Meg looked him in the face. "No," she said again.

"Yes. I came back to you, and I hurt you. I know I did. I just don't understand why."

"You came back, yes, but you didn't hurt me." He didn't, he hadn't, and in his weakness she didn't want him remembering who had. "You're confused, and no wonder. Your head…"

She couldn't do this. Couldn't lie and couldn't risk the truth. Leaning forward, she kissed him on the mouth. He sucked in a startled breath. Curling over her good leg, she sat back.

"I have to tell you something," she said.

His lids partially lowered, shielding his eyes as he watched her from behind his lashes. "This is going to be bad, isn't it?"

"No, not bad exactly. I don't think it's bad."

"Am I still welcome in your life, Meg? I was really looking forward to the springtime."

Meg started to cry in earnest. Half laughing, half weeping, she wiped futilely at the tears spilling down her cheeks.

"Hey, hey, now, enough. Come here."

He pulled her back down into the hospital bed with him. She curled both of her legs on the mattress, propping the casted ankle up on the good one. Beneath her cheek, his heart beat a little too rapidly.

"Are you okay?" she asked him, laying her hand on his chest.

"I'm really afraid you have something bad to tell me."

"Well, that depends on your point of view, I guess."

He stroked her hair across her crown, dipping forward to place a kiss on her forehead. The dampness of her tears soaked into his hospital gown. He grew still. "Go ahead."

She couldn't be sure he'd welcome the news, but she had to tell him, and now seemed as good a time as any, especially because it would divert his attention from the vague memories he appeared to be having about his possession by Matt. She drew a breath, and another, and a third before she blurted, "I'm pregnant."

He said nothing for a long moment before shifting his too-lean body on the narrow mattress. "Is that all?"

She sat up again. "All? What do you mean 'is that all'?"

"Well, I…I think I knew that. Didn't I?"

No, she thought. *Matt did.* "I don't see how," she said. "I just found out."

His brow furrowed. "I guess this is one of those things caused by the bleeding into my brain. The nurse told me about that. The wound to my head. I fell?"

"Yes. And I'm pregnant, okay? I mean, is that okay?"

"Is that okay?" he echoed. "With me, are you asking? It's fine with me. It's wonderful. But as I recall, you were afraid of having another child."

"I'm not afraid anymore."

Meg loosened his dark hair from around his bandage, smoothing it back. His gaze remained steady on hers, almost daring her to look away.

"Will you marry me?" he asked.

She wished she could stop crying long enough to answer him, but she couldn't, so she nodded instead.

"I might be in the hospital for a while, yet. When do you—"

Her fingers flew to his mouth and touched his lips. "In the springtime?"

"Yeah," said Caleb with a tired and beautiful grin spreading beneath her fingertips. "In the springtime."

Meet the Author

Celia Ashley lives in rural Lehigh County, Pennsylvania, an area rich in history and beauty and from which she has drawn inspiration for many of her tales. She is the mother of three grown sons, as well as the companion of four cats and one talkative parrot named Merlin. When not writing, she is a garden enthusiast (not an expert, by any means, but growing things makes her smile) and spends time painting in a variety of mediums. Published in historical romance under the pen names Alyssa Deane and Robin Maderich, she has most recently taken to writing spicy contemporary paranormal romance as Celia Ashley, for which she has received enthusiastic reviews. Ms. Ashley is a member of RWA and the Pocono-Lehigh Romance Writers chapter.